DANCING AT THE GOLD MONKEY

T0154564

DANCING AT THE GOLD MONKEY

Allen Learst

STORIES

Leapfrog Press
Fredonia, New York

Published in 2012 in the United States by
Leapfrog Press LLC
PO Box 505
Fredonia, NY 14063
www.leapfrogpress.com

Printed in the United States of America

Distributed in the United States by
Consortium Book Sales and Distribution
St. Paul, Minnesota 55114
www.cbsd.com

First Edition

ISBN: 978-1-935248-29-3

Library of Congress Cataloging-in-Publication Data

Learst, Allen.
  Dancing at the gold monkey : stories / Allen Learst. -- 1st ed.
    p. cm.
  ISBN 978-1-935248-29-3 (alk. paper)
  1. Vietnam War, 1961-1975--Veterans--Fiction. 2. Detroit
(Mich.)--Fiction. 3. Psychological fiction.
  I. Title.
  PS3612.E2376D36 2012
  813'.6--dc23

        2012027891

For my father

"I did not go crazy, not in the clinical sense,
but others did."
—Philip Caputo, *A Rumor of War*

ACKNOWLEDGEMENTS

Many people read and commented on these stories in their early manifestations. I want to thank you all for your unwavering patience, faith, and support, especially Lisa Graziano, Leapfrog Press publisher and editor whose keen eye and suggestions have made this a better book. I owe a debt of gratitude to Gordon Weaver and Ronald L. Johnson, the best friends and mentors a writer could have. Without their encouragement and editorial advice, I could not have found the voices to tell these stories. I also want to thank all the people who inspired these stories, the boys from the old neighborhood (you know who you are), my U.S. Department of Interior Fish and Wildlife friends and co-workers who liked what I wrote; and most of all, my comrades with whom I served in Vietnam—may you all find peace.

CONTENTS

DANCING AT THE GOLD MONKEY

UNDER ICE

It was spring at last. A breeze lifted fuzzy catkins from their branches; the boy watched them float to the ground. His father steered their 1957 Ford onto the asphalt driveway under gnarled maple trees; they passed beneath a stone arch, a wrought iron sign. "Pontiac State Hospital," it said. Their dark branches mingled with steel bars on the upper floor windows of several buildings bordering the drive. The Ford came to a halt in a parking space; the boy's father put the shifter into Park and said, "Will you be all right until I come out?"

"Sure," said the boy.

"Stay near the car, okay?"

"Okay."

The catkins crawled along the asphalt and crunched under the boy's shoes as he crossed the drive. He thought about caterpillars—the catkins reminded him; they'd made good bait. The steps leading into the building looked large and important. A woman sat by herself on a ledge near the doors. She held something wrapped in a blanket, rocking back and forth on the edge of the step.

A man trimmed hedges under windows alongside the building. Each hedge was cut uniformly across the top and it sides were squared. The boy liked how neat the hedges were, how they made him feel safe in a world where everything was crazy. He saw another man gather shovels and rakes and put them into a wheelbarrow. Two men stood nearby on the sidewalk; they looked like doctors; they talked and smoked cigarettes. One of the men kept turning his head to watch the woman at the top of the stairs. The other man said something and they both laughed.

On the bottom step, the boy took from his jacket a brand new Rappala fishing lure, and removed it from its little cardboard box; its hooks were silver and shiny. The long, thin iridescent minnow-like lure glimmered in the light as he moved it in a swimming motion. When he looked up, he noticed other people walking in a grassy area across the drive, and zipped his jacket against a chill coming on a cool wind. People walked arm in arm on the grass. A young man wiped his face with a handkerchief, held it to his eyes. The boy knew he must be crying; but he didn't know why—everything, the tall trees, the grass that looked like a golf course, the people who wore colorful clothes—it all looked so peaceful, like a park he'd once been to in Detroit before his family moved north to Caseville, when his mother laughed as she took chicken drums from a wicker basket and made them dance across the blanket; she loaded their plates with potato salad and baked beans. All day long the boy and his father had fished on the banks of the Detroit River, played catch on the grass, though his father often threw the ball too hard.

Not long after the picnic, when the arguments about moving to Caseville started, the boy heard his father tell his mother that she was nuts. Use your head, his father said; where would he find work? He was a city boy after all. Then his mother hurled a plate across the dining room table, where it smashed in blue and white pieces against Boston ivy wallpaper, and splintered across a hardwood floor. Finally, the arguments ended and they moved to Caseville; the boy was glad they were all going to live with his grandfather. How could this be bad? They would live near a lake, get to go swimming and fishing anytime they wanted. Wasn't it where they'd had their most summer fun? Didn't his father love going there for two weeks each summer, at Thanksgiving, and Christmas?

When winter arrived and the Huron Bay froze solid like a giant pearl, the boy followed his grandfather, Charlie, across the ice. He pulled his own sled loaded with minnow buckets and fishing gear. One time the boy's feet slipped out from under him, and he went down on the ice; his chin hit first. When he stood up, drops of blood splattered on the black ice. He fingered the cut and thought it might be bad. He caught up with his grandfather who was unlocking the door to the ice shanty and said, "I cut myself."

"Let me see," Charlie said.

"It hurts," he said, trying to hold back tears.

Inside the ice shanty his grandfather lit a lantern for warmth, and then broke through the ice, which had frozen over the hole since the last time they had fished. He took a handkerchief from his pocket and dipped it into the chilled water.

"Come closer," the old man said, as he scooped away some thin shards of ice with an ice ladle. He put them into a handkerchief and handed it to the boy. "Hold that on the cut. It'll be all right," he said.

Branches clacked in the wind. When he turned up his collar against a coming storm, the boy thought about how cold it was by the lake where he lived, especially since his grandfather had decided to take a trip to California to see his sister, Helen. Wind rattled his bedroom windows. He watched his breath steam from beneath a wool army blanket.

Firelight came through a crack in the door, flickered on the knotty pine paneling in the room where he slept. The knotholes seemed to watch him. He heard a door slam. His mother shouted, "I'm—not—crazy!"

"Be quiet," his father said.

He pulled the wool blanket close. He thought about the ice shanty; the lantern that gave off a warm glow, lighting the figure of his grandfather hunched over a hole in the ice.

"Look," his grandfather had said. A large northern pike swam by the dark green hole. His grandfather turned the lantern off so they could better see the bottom of the lake. The pike's fins rippled the sand as it swam past. He couldn't sleep so he thought about the spear his grandfather plunged into the hole, pinning the pike to the sand. Blood trailed in the water.

His mother came down the steps and stood near him. She didn't speak. The boy thought she looked pretty in her pale, blue dress; it matched her eyes. She stared at him. His father took him by the hand, and the three of them walked across the driveway to where the other hospital visitors had gathered. His father spread a blanket and his mother sat cross legged; the boy sprawled on the grass; his father lit a cigarette. "Can I have one of those?" his mother said. Her hand steadied his father's wrist, the match that shook to light her cigarette. They watched her smoke. He had never seen his mother smoke. She looked at him, as if studying him. "You're a good boy, I bet," she said, and then looked away. She looked up through the tree branches where some clouds gathered. "Can I go in now?" she said.

Maybe she remembered the night his father's voice woke him. Sleepy-eyed he went into the living room. "That goddamn oil stove doesn't work right!" his father said. "And I can't get this fireplace lit! It's always cold here."

"Son," his mother said, "Go get some kindling from the shed."

"He doesn't have to listen to you!" his father shouted.

His mother ran from the room. The boy took his winter coat from a hook on the back porch and laced his boots. They were still wet from playing outside earlier that day. He went out, passed the shed and woodpile; he walked north on the dead-end road where they lived. It was dark, but freshly fallen snow lit the way. At the end of the road, which wasn't far, he tried to remember all the details of the day his grandfather had lassoed a raccoon hiding in a tree trunk. The more he walked the more details came to him: "I've got something to show you. Get dressed," his grandfather whispered to him one morning.

It was early when he followed his grandfather into the frozen swamp. New snow fell during the night, and their feet crunched over dead cattails poking out of the snow. At the edge of the swamp they stopped at a gnarled tree with a hole in it. The boy's grandfather took thick leather gloves from his backpack and put them on. He reached into the hole and pulled out a young raccoon by its neck, clinched tight in his huge fist. He looped the rope around the raccoon's neck and gave the rope to the boy. The raccoon pulled hard against his small hands; it snarled, but the sound didn't scare the boy. The dog they called Tarzan yelped and snapped at the cowering raccoon. His grandfather laughed.

His mother stopped at the top of the steps and turned toward him. His father held her hand and brushed his lips across her cheek. He said something the boy couldn't hear. His face looked like clay. She looked down at him, then turned and walked into the building. Large wooden and glass doors closed behind her with a dull thud. His father said, "Please get in the car, Son."

The woman the boy had been watching earlier clutched her blanket. No one paid much attention to her. She rocked on the steps. "If that dirty bastard ever does that again I'll. . . ."

His father turned to follow his mother inside, but didn't look at the woman.

Before his mother stopped talking, and his grandfather had been gone for two months just before Christmas, the three of them sat at the kitchen table eating dinner. The pull-down lamp hung close over their heads and spread its yellow light in a circle on the table. The burners on a gas stove were lit. Blue flames sputtered there. The oven door was open. Three bowls steamed toward the light. His father stared into his soup. "Everywhere I look I see nothing but goddamn fish scales," his father said. "Fish scales on the table, fish scales on my spoon, fish scales in my coffee."

The boy thought his father was funny. He giggled. "Fish scale soup," he said.

"It's a good thing your grandfather decided to

22

pull out for the winter, or we'd have to turn this place into a fish house."

"Clean fish every day," the boy said.

"I'd rather fall through the ice and drown," his father said. "It's a sweet death."

"Harold. . . ." The boy's mother said. "Think about the boy."

"Grandpa says you can't drown in the lake," the boy said.

"People get trapped under the ice all the time and die there," his father said.

"Grandpa says you can find pockets at the surface and stay under the ice for a long time. Like Houdini."

His father got up from the table and poured himself and his wife a cup of coffee. "Houdini is just a legend, Son. That means the story isn't real. Houdini would have frozen to death if that were true," his father said.

"My baby's gone," the boy's mother said, staring blankly through the boy.

His father reached across the table and put his hand on her shoulder. "I know," he said.

When the boy closed the car door and looked across a long expanse of lawn toward a different building, bars covered the window panes and looked like black icicles; the boy saw a shadow pass one of the windows; then the figure returned and stood there. He wanted to leave this place and never come back; he wanted his mother to be at home when they got there; instead, in the rearview mirror he saw the same two men he'd seen on the sidewalk earlier. They took hold of the woman who'd sat on the steps; each man had a hold of an arm. They said something to her and pulled her to her feet. She shook her head furiously, and then they all went inside. The boy opened the glove box and took out a *Sports Afield*; he turned each page until he found two men standing on a frozen lake. Piles of fish were scattered about them. One man held up a stringer of big perch, a huge smile on his face beneath a black and red checkered hat. Someday, the boy thought, that would be him and his grandfather. They would be in a magazine, too.

One night the boy asked when his grandfather would be coming home. His father looked up from his newspaper and said, "He doesn't want us here," then stared at the boy's mother who sat in a rocking chair.

She rocked faster. "I wanted to take care of him. That's all there was to it," she said.

"Christ, Maggie!" The boy's father said. "The

old bird's in California most of the winter, while we freeze our asses off up here."

"I wanted to take care of him when he was here. He needed me." Shivering, his mother rose from the rocker. Taking the poker from where it leaned against the fireplace, she hooked a log and pulled it into the coals where it would burn better. She went back to the rocker and pulled the knitted afghan around her shoulders.

"If we went back to the city I could get a decent job, take care of you and the boy. You wouldn't be so cold then," he said.

The boy sat on the floor near the fireplace, and wrapped a braided line on two bent nails driven into the handle of a homemade fishing pole. The rocking chair squeaked across the hardwood floor.

"He doesn't do anything around here except go fishing," his father said.

"Go to bed, Son," his mother said.

The car door opened. The boy's father slid in behind the wheel. He started the car and backed out of the parking space. The boy watched him. "Why are there bars on those windows?" The boy said.

"To keep sick people in," his father said.

"Are they prisoners?"

"No."

The Ford crossed shadows on the driveway in

front of one building where the boy's mother was kept. He looked through the car window and followed one of the shadows from the ground up to the third floor, and saw his mother. She stood in one of the windows, divided by panes of crooked glass. The boy waved to her. Slowly, she raised her hand and waved. She was smiling.

The car exited through the stone gateway and picked up speed on the highway. The boy fell asleep. When he woke he remembered a dream he wanted to tell his father but decided he would not. In his dream he was walking on the ice with his grandfather; through his breath, he saw an ice shanty in the distance. They kept walking, but the shanty never got closer. He turned to ask his grandfather about the shanty, but his grandfather was gone. Then he fell through a hole in the ice. The hole closed over him. He struggled, pushed against the ice; he was sinking until he heard a voice say, "Drowning is the sweetest death." Air escaped his lungs; he followed the bubbles upward to the underside of ice where his mouth found a pocket of air. Breathing heavily, he saw the distorted figure of his mother's face as she bent to kiss him.

A KISS

Randy Kodoski sits in Strohshiems listening to one factory rat tell another a joke about a guy who finds a genie in a bottle. The guy wishes for a twelve-inch prick but ends up with a little man on his shoulder who runs up and down the bar kicking over drinks. All Kodoski wants is a cigarette. Kodoski throws a dollar on the bar, leaves the cool of Strohshiems, and walks out into the midday sun.

Down the block there's a mom and pop once owned by Micky's mother and father, and Kodoski doesn't recognize the men standing behind an inch of Plexiglas though he's been in the store several times. Towel heads. One of them, the darker, wears a T-shirt. *Detroit*, it says, *No Place for Wimps.* The other, skinny to the bone, says, "How you today, sir?"

Kodoski says, "Pack of Kools."

Micky's father opened his store at seven a.m. then worked the Chrysler Plant day shift, and

Micky's grandmother, wearing an ankle-length cotton dress and babushka, even in the summer, came to sit on her rocker in the corner, and his mother spoke Polish to her, but Micky couldn't understand, except for a few cuss words, and he refused to even try because he thought it was stupid, but he'd bring the old woman drinks from the cooler.

Micky'd say, "Let's get away from these dumb Polacks and go have a smoke in the alley."

Before leaving the store, Kodoski notices the bony one's purple shirt, wide collar, the first three buttons unbuttoned and a gold chain on a hairy chest. He doesn't like it. Outside the mom and pop, Kodoski spots a hundred by the curb. No reason to get excited. He picks Franklin from the hot pavement, smoothes him against his thigh and tucks him away. The sun drops behind the Penobscot building and the Renaissance Center.

An orange sky.

Looks like home.

On the next block, Kodoski pushes a button and hears a buzzer. Dom doesn't allow hippies or junkies, and you'd think the club is private, but it's not, just selective.

Two ceiling fans hum over the bar, and photographs of Joe Louis, Rocky Marciano, and local

Homeboy LaCroix, "Golden Gloves Champion of Detroit" with his arms raised and fists clenched. Dom's a big man, former boxer, but now he likes whiskey and cigars, one hanging from his lip. His cheeks are puffed and he breathes hard. He makes a left-handed jab at Kodoski. "What's a matter with you?" Dom says.

"Seen Micky?"

"Mickiewicz don't come lately," Dom says, "maybe trying out new pussy now his old lady's got work."

It won't work Jean said when she showed him Micky's letter, the one saying he'd be home in two weeks, and not hiding it either in the box from Thom McCann's under the bed with Micky's other letters she didn't think anyone knew were there, except for Kodoski who didn't understand Micky was crazy for Jean until he read them, and then she was gone, and a woman gone is good, Kodoski thinks, means you had one to lose, and he can't remember one staying long enough to call his old lady, but he's sure, as sure as he's standing there talking to Dom, his luck will change as he slaps his money on the bar. Kodoski needs a break from the Polack geezers, every day at Dom's to play cards and drink boilermakers; he can get things moving with Micky's help.

Over the bar, on a TV, an 11-year-old boy drills a hole through his head. Russian roulette. A cop sorry about a missing gun. Two men, a liquor store robbed. An old woman, raped and murdered. Nixon says the war is over. Dom holds Franklin to the light, and says, "You find work?"

"Takes two arms," says Kodoski. All he wants is pocket money and he'll stand in the unemployment line as long as it takes, wait for his disability to come in the mail each month, cash his checks at Strohshiems and shoot eight ball at Ma's Pool Hall. He's thinking he'll slide a piece of green inside Jasmine's G-string, a dancer at the Gold Monkey, barely nineteen. Jean won't live with him no matter what he promises; she's too smart for him, too in love with him he's sure and Micky's his best friend.

Dom waves when Kodoski hits the door. Kools in his pocket, the solid feel of a Zippo warm against free currency. He's two minutes from the Monkey. Kodoski's across the street, passing a billboard for Chance Bail Bonds and Ma's Pool Hall, blinds drawn, lights low, mom and pop just around the corner—a skinny towel head catching shit for losing his hard-earned bread.

Worse can happen.

Has happened.

A KISS

Someone might come in with a 12-gauge. The darker one will try polite, not look up, say, "Sir, can I help?" Skinny one bolts for the pisser, his blood smeared on a cooler door advertising Strohs six-packs for $3.79, tugging the gold chain around his neck. The darker, eyes wide. "Take, you take," he'll say. "Take," then the slide action one more time; then it's quiet. A sucking chest wound. A flicker of neon. The night blue like night on film.

Inside the Gold Monkey, Kodoski's adjusting to light and palms two bucks to Farmer Jack, a short hairy man without a shirt and wearing coveralls, an iguana tattoo slithering down his forearm. Farmer Jack says, "Micky's looking for you."

Oh Suzy Q, baby I love you. . . .

Jasmine lap dances for a fat biker who wants to touch her headlights but it's against the rules. Farmer Jack will bounce him in a beat.

Before it was the Gold Monkey and you had to stick money in that place between Jasmine's navel and muff because you couldn't resist her tight ass in your face, Kodoski's father gave him nickels to play "Pretty Woman" on the juke box at Frank Deluca's restaurant. Before the walls were red velvet and the room filled with smoke, Kodoski's father said, when his mother ordered fish and chips, only a dago like Frank made spaghetti the way it was supposed to be and everyone laughed, including Frank who came to their table to ask: "Everything's a good, no?"

Kodoski sits at the bar and orders boilermakers from Miss Schenk, who's wearing a leopard skin leotard over a gut-sprung middle. "Let's hear it for Jasmine!" Miss Schenk shouts.

Then Jasmine has her arms around Kodoski; he feels her breasts against his shoulder, the odor of cheap perfume, but Kodoski's looking at the fading light behind Farmer Jack in the doorway; he sees rain hit the sidewalk in little explosions; he sees the shadows of other men—Homeboy LaCroix is one of them—waiting for the next dancer, and Farmer Jack coming toward him, big and hairy, smelling like a locker room, carrying something in a brown paper bag heavy with humidity; he hears Farmer Jack say, "You need one of these?" and opens the bag.

Maybe he's had too much to drink too early, Kodoski thinks, but you had to appreciate a .45, its chromed steel heavy and secure, like the one in Nam he gave Sergeant Tiner twenty-five bucks for, a drunk from Detroit he barely knew and didn't like, could care less if he drank himself to death, but only wanted him to pass out before the gun he waved in front of his face went off inside a hooch at Phu Bai almost killing Micky, who was there too, looking wide-eyed at the hole in the floor where the bullet passed between his legs two weeks before Tiner returned to the states and the neighborhoods Kodoski thought he'd never see again.

"You be around later, honey?" Jasmine says.

He's looking into Jasmine's cleavage, wishing he had a whiskey dick; that's what Micky called a hard-on that wouldn't quit, but this isn't one of those times. Then Jasmine disappears in a red glow behind the stage.

All Farmer Jack wants is thirty bucks to calm his shakes, and hands over the bag. Kodoski sticks it under his fatigue jacket where the hard feel of it nudges his Zippo, the weight of it pressing him into a bar stool, his mind like helium from too many boilermakers. Kodoski's arm throbs like it did the night he left it in a foxhole when NVA ran over Firebase Henderson.

Orange Vietnam sunset.

Blue South China Sea.

Kodoski heard, as he drifted in and out of consciousness, Micky calling his name. A rat on hind legs. Heard someone say, "Over here." Something in its mouth. Heard too many voices become one voice shouting for a medic. Whiskers against eyelids. He smelled the meat packing plant at the

Eastern Market where his father worked every day for most of his life, and came home with ground meat tied neatly in long bundles of white packing paper, slick on one side to keep it from sticking, like the gauze did wrapped around his arm when the morphine wore off that first time on the hospital ship in Cam Rhan Bay.

Miss Schenk says, "Where you goin'?"

"Business," says Kodoski, and he rises from the bar stool and makes for the rear door.

Kodoski walks into the alley behind the Gold Monkey; he's on his way to Ma's Pool Hall, the orange sunset only a memory in the dark sky. His own shadow lost in others that crawl along fences, the trash bins near the edge of concrete, moving blades of grass and weeds where Jean waits for him to come into a light he'll never understand. Bare bulbs illuminate rear entrances to Dom's and Chance Bail Bonds. The street lit by lamplight no longer familiar to him.

Kodoski's sure Micky will be waiting at Ma's, just as he's convinced the pain in his arm is real, and then remembers when he'd asked Jean to rub the phantom arm for him one night when he forgot himself, when he'd smoked too much dope, mixed it with whiskey, and Jean recoiled like a rifle, and the expression on her face, not one of sympathy or even pity, but of fear, made him think he'd gone too far.

The pool hall is empty when Kodoski walks in. Dust motes and smoke from Ma's cigarette drift in the light over faded green tables, and Ma, mostly in shadow, sits in an overstuffed chair in the corner, her dark skin barely visible. "What say you, young Kodoski?" says Ma, learning forward in the light, her form outlined against the wall. She's the biggest woman Kodoski's ever seen. "You lookin' for Micky, ain't you?" Ma is too big to move. "Bring me a Coke."

It was always Ma's Pool Hall: the same ticking clock on a shelf above the red cooler, Coke written in white sweeping letters across the front; pool cues at attention in the rack against the wall. It was Ma's when the plaster, still smooth and white, glistened when she pulled the blinds, letting in the light, and Ma weighed one hundred and fifteen pounds, and waited for one of the sixty-six black airmen, a good looking man she called Daddy, who never came home, who sat in the back of a bus on a long ride to Tuskegee, Alabama, not knowing in two years he'd go down in a P-51 Mustang somewhere in North Africa.

But Ma was still there after the war, when a soda cost a nickel and Kodoski's father played pool, and Kodoski's mother left Frank Deluca's restaurant where she worked in the late afternoon, twenty years old, wearing a blue chiffon dress that first time, the one without sleeves his father said he could see right through when the sun was behind her, and her standing on the sidewalk just as he came out of Ma's, cigarettes rolled in his T-shirt, and a few dollars he'd won on a table; it was the first time she'd have a drink with him.

"You've seen Micky?" Kodoski says.

"I seen a lot of things," says Ma. "Could be I seen Micky. He got too many troubles this night. How Ma know that? She tell you when you kiss her," and puts a finger to her lips.

She edges forward in the light, and Kodoski sees a speck of ceiling plaster on her bare shoulder, near the strap holding the cloth covering her like a tent, her milky white eyes larger in the light, red veins closing in on her dark pupils, the quivering flesh of her throat. "Ma ain't gonna hurt you, soldier boy."

Kodoski smells lavender and cigarettes, and something's lodged in Kodoski's throat he can't move. Ma cradles his head, her hands smooth against his cheeks, the touch of her palms like paper or wax, like his mother's hands felt the night he woke to a kiss, her cool lips pressed against the cold sweat on his forehead, and his mother saying, "You're home. You're home," because he was gasping for air and half conscious, the bed sheets heavy as fallen beams and earth. Then Ma's mouth is wet on his lips. "Ma knows things," she says, and leans back in the big chair, Kodoski inhaling the air around her as if it were only enough for him.

The glass doors to Ma's Pool Hall rattle when Kodoski opens them, and before stepping into the street and closing the doors behind him, the old woman lights another cigarette, her face glowing in the darkness around her. "You gonna see like Ma," she says. "Gabriel's. That's where Micky's goin'."

On the sidewalk, heading for Gabriel's, Kodoski runs his tongue across his lips and tastes sweet cola and cigarettes. He understands possibilities. He'll make his way the four blocks, past Dom's, the Gold Monkey, and he'll see Dom standing in the doorway, the geezers, unsteady, going home, a blue neon Pabst sign lighting their way out of the Dom Polski Club. Kodoski will wonder if he's like them, able to see clearly the life before him, every night at Dom's, the Gold Monkey, or Gabriel's.

"Goodnight, Dom."

"Goodnight, fellas."

"Goodnight."

Kodoski's got money rolled in his pocket, a half pack of Kools, an automatic in his belt he's sure Micky's going to appreciate. Micky can get things moving. Kodoski will ask him how it is with Jean, and knowing there's no answer, Kodoski will see it doesn't matter.

Dark streets.

Humid night air.

He'll see a lot of things: Maybe Miss Schenk and Farmer Jack will leave the Gold Monkey to check on a baby in the apartment they share with Miss Schenk's mother, who's just fourteen years older than Miss Schenk, and who'll ask for money to have one drink at Gabriel's before it closes; maybe the darker towel head will be home in bed with his wife, thinking about the hundred dollar bill his brother lost, and his brother, the skinny one, might be dreaming about a place he no longer remembers, asking polite questions in the dream: "Please, sir. Where am I?" and Ma, asleep in the big chair, will spill a coke in her lap, soaking the crotch of her dress, and then go to the canopied bed she's slept in since it was Ma's Pool Hall, and fall asleep until she dreams about the young pilot who never came home, and even if Micky's not at Gabriel's like Ma said, he's sure to come.

A SHEET, A CLOTHESLINE, A BED

August 15, 1970

What is it? I don't know. It comes nearer. My toes dig into cool sand. I'm so goddamned stoned. Earlier, at the perimeter. Black cloth hanging from barbed wire. A gook kid. You get us dinky dao? We buy from you? No sweat, GI. You number fucking one, GI. A green patch floats on the South China Sea, but looks white to me until I know it's green because Mr. Brown says so. Is white a primary color? The absence of color? The whole world gone white. White out. Flashback from Hawaiian acid I took on R and R. Yes, the absence of color. Yes. A sail from a Vietnamese fishing boat. Mr. Brown doesn't think so. "It's a fucking parachute," Homeboy says. I look at Mr. Brown and Homeboy. Now they are all colors: black silhouettes and elongated shadows streaking across the beach. I love them. I love the gook kid who brings us weed. Mr. Brown says, "Made of silk, ain't it?" Yes. Silk. Like farting through silk, my father said each payday. "Worth beaucoup dope," says Homeboy. Beaucoup: much, many. I love them beaucoup.

The chute—a sheet in the wind, the water a clothesline, a bed—nears the shore, and Homeboy says, "Wade out and get it, Mr. Brown." Floating. Rolling. Colors in Mr. Brown's brown eyes in the whites of his eyes say, "You fucking crazy, man. Sharks out there." Mr. Brown's brown eyes say sharks out there, man. Now green nylon cords spread like tentacles from a Portuguese man-of-war. Sting the shit out of you. Only cure is piss on the welts. Unraveling, untangling. Mr. Brown's brown arms pull on the nylon cords. Water laps his legs. "Something inside," Mr. Brown shouts. A fish?

. . .bloated . . . man . . . pilot. Words in the surf. The silk unmakes itself into a fighter pilot stuffed into a G-suit. American. Homeboy says, "Jesus Christ." Rubbery skin. Gray hands. Mr. Brown says: "I need help." Fat white man. Poor fat dead white man. His head a green helmet—his eyes covered by a sun visor. Homeboy says we need to turn him loose, drag that white boy up on the beach so his mama can have him back. Dead fighter pilot boy whose mama wants him back. Mr. Brown rolls that dead fighter up on the beach, pulls the silk behind, loosens the cords from his feet. In a few hours military police will remove his helmet, his visor no longer shading his dead eyes, his suit unzipped, his dog tags removed; one gleams Robert Spendlove when the MP says his name under Vietnam moonlight. Where are Mr. and Mrs. Spendlove tonight? "Holy shit," Homeboy says. "Did you see Robert's face?" Robert's face is wrinkled, and his eyes like shriveled grapes looking at Homeboy. Holy shit.

July 21, 1973

Where are we? We're with these two chicks from the neighborhood. Both good fucks. They're upstairs in my apartment. Nothing special. Cheap. I rent from Ma. She owns a pool hall downstairs. We're downstairs in Ma's Pool Hall. She sells beer and wine, sometimes hard stuff. Ma likes me and Mr. Brown. We're cool. She says, "Who you got up there?" Ma is closed, blinds drawn, lights out. Her fat hangs over the arms of her chair, droops from her face. Legs too heavy to move. Mr. Brown smiles that big white Mr. Brown smile. "Some girls," he says. Girls. Yes. "Women, Mr. Brown. Women," says Ma. Dago Girl and Peroxide, Mr. Brown calls them. Peroxide's big blue Polack eyes,

cleavage. Dago Girl's nipples. Jet black hairs growing out of them. Two girls sipping Jim Beam. Two
girls waiting for Mr. Brown and me.

Ma doesn't ask about the war, but she asks about
Homeboy. "Prison," I say. "Jackson for busting up
a white man." Bar fight. A broken white man. Too
long ago. Ma only says: "Poor Homeboy." Her
eyes follow Mr. Brown to the back room where
she keeps her stash. "Where'd you get that name,
Mr. Brown?" says Ma. From Homeboy. Mr. Brown
from Detroit town. "My real name's Toby. Tobias
Jones." Jim Beam and beer in Mr. Brown's brown
hand. Upstairs. Yes. Peroxide says, "Mr. Brown, you
one pretty brown man." A ceiling fan. Detroit heat
around a pretty brown man. Dago Girl drops ice
into glasses. Mr. Brown pours Jim Beam. Peroxide
says, "It feels good," squeezes Mr. Brown's thigh.
"All of us getting to know each other this way."
Mr. Brown's hand slides up a red skirt to creamy
white panties. Knowing. A hard cock against Peroxide's leg. Ice clinks in glasses. Dago Girl's hand
inside my shirt. She says, "Come in here." Now
Peroxide and Mr. Brown follow Dago Girl into the
bedroom. Zippers. Undressing. A white sheet. A
bed for Mr. Brown and me. Dago Girl's perfumed
hair. Mr. Brown's sweat. White arms and brown
legs unweave a tangled sheet. Where are we? The

apartment. Yes. A tongue on Dago Girl's nipple, fingers around Mr. Brown's cock, a thigh pressed between Peroxide's legs, Mr. Brown's brown hand on white ass. Dago Girl says, "Touch all of me." Breathing. Mr. Brown untwists the sheet from Peroxide's long legs, pulls her onto the floor, sets her free of the bed. "Oh God," she says. Laughing. She takes Mr. Brown's brown hand, leads him to the bath, and then a shower curtain slides. Closes. Water. I'm so goddamned drunk. Oh God.

December 16, 1976

Where does he go? Nowhere. What I know is this: Homeboy is put into a cell across from a man he calls One-Eyed Crane. In his third year at Jackson, Homeboy kills him. Yes. Unknowing. Kills him.

What I imagine is this: Crane lying on a bed, staring through the blackness at Homeboy. He sees everything with one blue eye, reads Homeboy's lips; he knows when a deal goes down, shivers under his sheet. Excited. Homeboy warns him: "Motherfucker," he says, "if your eye offends me, I'll pluck it out." Crane loves Homeboy's mouth. Thick lips. Pink inside. He loves to watch it in the dark. Yes. In the night, Homeboy's lips say, "Look brother, dope for beaucoup green." A white face, a uniform, a nightstick. "Don't cross me, boy," it says. Betrayed. No reason. A deal gone wrong. Homeboy finds Crane in a prison laundry room.

"Christ," Crane says, "the nigger's got me." A sheet around his head. A cord around his neck. One eye loose from its socket. Crane's dead—Homeboy his killer. Jesus.

I know it's close to Christmas because lights strung around a tree look white to me until she says, "I love the colors. They're beautiful, aren't they?" Her name is Nurse; the lights in Nurse's eyes say, "Do you like the ornaments? Can I bring you anything?" Beautiful. Ornaments. Cigarettes. I love this pretty white nurse who brings me cigarettes. Beaucoup cigarettes. Yes. She doesn't ask about Homeboy, but shows Mr. Brown where to find me. Veteran's hospital. Detroit. Mr. Brown works at Ford's now. He comes to see me, tells me he methodically stacks numbered parts with a fork lift in a warehouse called Bondage Stores. He wants to know when I'll leave the hospital. He has a pretty brown wife, a little brown boy. "Mr. Brown," I say, "just light this cigarette for me."

PLACES PART DREAM

The life Bobby Spendlove and Cheryl Martens know in Key West is one of palm trees bristling in breezes off Gulf waters, tourists gathering for sunset celebrations at Mallory Square, and tarpon cruising the pier for cut-bait cleaned from the docks at Garrison's Marina. Great Blue Herons and flamingos wade the shallows for smaller fish and mollusks, and Black Skimmers, their lower beaks extended, trace lines through the water.

Bobby and Cheryl have been together the entire day. It's their high school graduation. Class of '68. It's late afternoon on Higgs Beach. The gang's coolers are spread across the sand. Empty. Their voices quiet, volleyball nets abandoned. Cheryl and Bobby go for one last swim. She puts her tongue in Bobby's mouth, slips her hand down his trunks. He lowers the straps of her swimsuit, feels her nipple grow hard between his fingers. "I love you, Bobby," Cheryl says.

Bobby likes the taste of her mouth, the spot between her legs warmer than the Gulf. When he comes, Bobby says, "I love you, too."

Bobby's thinking he won't be a boy for long. He's joined the U.S. Navy. Soon he'll be wearing a crisp white uniform, brass buttons gleaming like the sun. He'll be an officer. "You'll be kicking gook ass before you know it," the recruiter said. He's going to be a pilot, a lieutenant no doubt, and maybe, once he's flown enough missions, a captain.

Sitting close to Bobby on the ride home, Bobby shifting gears, racing the engine as he slows for the turn into her drive, Cheryl sees the sun edging the horizon. Purple clouds laced with orange. She's thinking about Bobby's friends—boys who can't wait to be men. These boys, including Bobby, are easy targets, easy to tease. At the beach they side-stepped to her like scolded pups looking for affection, for approval, like they wanted to get close to her, hoping she'd take note of their hard bodies, the outline of cock inside their swimsuits. She noticed, but ignored them. She knows it's a part she's expected to play, a script she reads from when she's cued. She has the lead, determines the plot. She kisses Bobby goodnight, tells him to call.

Bobby feels spent, tired form a long day of volleyball, drinking beers, and fucking. He's proud to have a chick like Cheryl, the envy of all the guys. These moments make him feel good, when his world slows and he sees everything ahead happening the way he intends it to. Instead of his Chevy Nova, Bobby can visualize himself strapped inside the cockpit of an F4, the Navy's most sophisticated fighter. The name on his helmet will read "Shark" or "Stingray." There will be photographs he'll mail home to Cheryl and his two best friends, Carter and Taylor.

They'll appreciate the radar guided Sparrow missiles he'll have at the touch of his finger; he'll see flashes on the ground, hear jet engines roar as he climbs at mach speed to avoid anti-aircraft, putting distance between himself and the enemy. On Cheryl's street, Bobby guns the Nova's engine, burns rubber in two gears and races home, thinking of the stories he'll have to tell when he's back from the war.

Exhausted, Cheryl collapses on her bed, stares at Davy Jones and the Beatles smiling back from a wall painted pink. She's too tired to shower, a thin film of sea salt covering her body. She feels different, like an adult, like there are more possibilities for her future than she can run through her mind. Though she wonders why Bobby's decided to join the Navy, Cheryl has her own dreams, an inner life. The inner life of Cheryl Martens. Yet something is nagging her. Bobby's too smart for the military. Is that it? He could be anything. Couldn't he? An engineer. A lawyer, like her father, who's making her go to college next year, after she's saved enough money of her own, after she's learned responsibility. Bobby'll make money at whatever he does. She's convinced. Then they'll be married.

Bobby is sure to want children, too. They'll be blond and sturdy like him. Every night she'll make him dinner, put on the lingerie he'll buy for her. On Saturdays they'll lie in bed all day, go dancing at night. But what if Bobby doesn't want to marry her? What if he meets someone else? Maybe a girl on a naval base where he's assigned. Maybe a Vietnamese girl. That will certainly be a waste. Won't it? For sure.

Then there's college. Why should she wait for Bobby to make up his mind? Why the Navy instead of her in the first place? Her thoughts are confusing; her plans for the future a vague onionskin sketch, one of the possible overlays of a life yet to be imagined. Lying in the bed she's slept in for ten of her eighteen years, Cheryl decides she's just going to let her life happen; she's not at all worried.

Bobby parks the Nova, walks across the dew-heavy lawn in front of his house, anxious to sleep, to dream about flying.

Anything's possible in a war. Carter and Taylor, who can't believe he's balling a fox like Cheryl, will quit asking, "Why?" when they see him in uniform, see the ribbons over his heart. When he's serving his country, Taylor will be flexing his muscles for the Cuban pussy he says doesn't interest him, thinking how he's going to get into Cheryl's pants. Without a doubt.

And Carter's old man, who knows a good shrink up in Miami, will get his kid out of the draft. Taylor's going to put peanut butter up his ass, declare himself a homosexual. Those faggots, Bobby thinks, will be working concessions at Zachary State Park. They'll have snotty brats hanging off them before they know what hit them.

Climbing the steps to the veranda, where Bobby's mother and father are watching the sun go down, gulls like penciled Ws against deep blue, Bobby's sure that's no life for him. No life at all.

Staring wide-eyed at her bedroom ceiling, light fading outside with the sunset, Cheryl can't believe how much she's changed, how at first she wouldn't let Bobby touch her in those places he wanted to, not until their senior year, when he took her on his father's boat, the *Millie Jean.* Maybe it was the sound of the engines slicing the waves, the wind in her hair on the flying bridge, or the dolphins playing in the boat's wake that made her want to take off her top, squeeze between Bobby and the wheel, put his hands on her breasts. She knew she'd made Bobby feel like a man. That first time with Bobby might have even turned into pleasure if he hadn't rolled off her so quickly, then asked her to swim. Touching herself under the sheet, Cheryl thinks: What would it be like with someone else?

Bobby pauses; he hears his mother and father talking. They sit in a porch swing, the sun behind them dipping into the ocean, a light coming off the water as if it will never happen again. Bobby knows his mother. She has that same look she always has, those round blue eyes set in a child's worried face, the look he saw when he jumped from the veranda, when he fell like a stone, a blur in the hot and humid Florida sun. He was ten years old and glued together cardboard wings, thinking he could fly.

He saw his mother run from the house that time, saw her standing over him, a small thin woman who wouldn't see him cry, would only see his arm twisted, unnatural, broken.

"He's a dreamy boy," Bobby hears his mother say.

His father, sipping a daiquiri, says, "Don't fret so, Millie."

"He's such a part of me, but outside of me. A boy like Bobby. . . ."

"Johnson says it'll be over soon."

"Not soon enough."

Cheryl cannot imagine the stranger she'll meet at Sloppy Joe's. She's there to wait for a friend who's supposed to meet her but never arrives. She'll be home from college, sit next to a boy in uniform taking the long way home from Vietnam because he isn't ready to go home, and reveal a secret to him after too many drinks. She'll try not to think about Bobby, the baby she's aborted. Bobby's child. A foolish thing. One afternoon at Higgs Beach.

"I'm not a kid anymore," she'll say.

This man, long sideburns, hair at his collar,

face symmetrical, says, "I can see that." He's calm behind wire-rimmed glasses. Cheryl laughs. At him? At herself? The sound comes from outside of her it seems, as if it's someone else's laugh she hears, unfamiliar to her. That same night she'll ask his name. "I'm Ray," he says. "From Michigan." She'll go with Ray to a motel and lie naked with him, let him fill her, let him rock her to a rhythm only she can decide. She won't think about Bobby dead, only a flag for his mother to hold.

Who is a boy like Bobby? Bobby thinks. A boy like Bobby has model airplanes spinning from his bedroom ceiling, framed posters of fighter jets engaged in scenes of combat, flying low in formation over rice paddies. A boy like Bobby thinks about his father who was in the war, who shipped out of Pearl Harbor two days before the Japs bombed it, and another time drifted at sea for three days with two other sailors before being rescued, came home a commissioned officer with a Bronze Star and Purple Heart.

Afterwards, his father made enough money selling insurance to buy a forty-five-foot Ray Davis Sportfisherman he named the *Millie Jean*. Then he taught Bobby how to pilot, how to guide

the boat out of her slip at Key West bight, brag-
ging to his friends how lucky he was to have a
son much older than his years. Like a little adult
his father was fond of saying to his friends, and
would ask his wife, "How old was he then, Millie?
Thirteen? Fourteen?"

But a man like Bobby, Bobby thinks, slipping
past his parents, down the hall to the kitchen for
a bowl of cereal, knows the ocean better than his
father, understands tides and currents, where to
catch swordfish when his father's not there to tell
him. It was the natural order of things. Wasn't it?
Did a fish understand its own motion the way
he, Bobby, understands the life before him? Did
the swordfish know its own power, its ability to
turn on a dime, feed on other fish or defend itself when it had to? Even sharks were afraid of
them. Would it be the same for him when he was
a pilot?

When he's almost asleep, Bobby's become that
pilot. He taxis into position on the USS Ranger
for takeoff during a night mission. He will feel
the catapult launch initiate, the flight deck underneath giving way to the jet's thrust.

He's on a mission, one of the first fighter
squadrons to bomb Haiphong during Operation
Rolling Thunder. He's imagined it, but something

is wrong, terribly wrong. One of his afterburners will go out; he will be advised by the control tower to turn around. The sun is six degrees below the horizon—twilight. He will gain altitude, and then quickly lose it, feeling himself fall. His Radar Intercept Officer, Lieutenant Bill Wright, will sequence the ejection system one mile from the ship. Bill Wright will be rescued.

Bobby will hear his spine snap when he's exploded from the cockpit, his arms flailing as he drops from the sky. When the earth rises to meet him, the ocean will pull him down. He'll hear choppers searching the waves, the last of his thoughts disappearing under foreign waters he doesn't understand.

Cheryl will want Ray to hold her. That's all. She'll live in Key West for the rest of her life long after her divorce from Ray, only once in a while remembering a boy named Bobby. She'll be married again after Ray tells her his real life is in Michigan, and she'll have a son by her second husband she names Robert: she'll let Robby go through the attic where Cheryl's high school memories are buried in a box her little boy will find. "Who's this, Mom," he will ask, pointing to the photographs Cheryl showed to Ray once when he asked to see them. It seemed to Cheryl that everything changed then; she should have never mentioned them; she should have never made Ray feel as though he had been competing with a dead man, an officer in the U.S. Navy. It was as if her memories of Bobby Spendlove were part of a life innocent and pure, and she couldn't give them up.

But for her son she'll dust off the ones she's kept in plastic bamboo-like frames next to her bureau, put away in a box she'd forgotten. There is one of Bobby standing on a pier, an aircraft carrier in the background; Bobby in the cockpit of a fighter jet; Bobby on a flight deck with his buddies. They're all so young.

Cheryl will wish she could reach into one of the photos and pull Bobby back home, thinking of the day when the news came, praying then every day it wouldn't come, sensing the whole time Bobby was away it was going to happen, as if it already had.

Bobby's high school graduation picture will remind her of a day at Higgs Beach so long ago. She won't tell her new husband Bobby came home in a closed casket, not that he'd ask; she won't make the same mistake she made with Ray, but she'll share this with her son and say, "It was as if he'd never come home at all." It was as if he'd never existed except for the memories buried with all the other people she'd known, and all the events she experienced in a place part dream and part reality.

SHADOWBOXING

One February night Homeboy LaCroix killed a man in the Gold Monkey. He only meant to hurt him. When Homeboy struck with a left jab followed by a hard right, the man's head snapped back and his neck made a cracking sound. Then Homeboy left the Monkey and nobody tried to stop him. On the street he saw his breath in the cold air. His leather coat hung too heavy on his shoulders. Homeboy's pace quickened under a sky dark with clouds. A slender woman with long straight hair crossed the street, avoiding his eyes.

Then Mai was walking on a beach—a warm breeze from the South China Sea moved under her silk *ao dai*, her charcoal hair lifting in a current of air. But that was a long time ago.

He was a boxer. He did time at the Kronk Recreation Center, working up a good sweat—the shots he took and the ones he gave was how he got rid of the shit. Stacked so hard and high you had to beat it down. Mai embroidered gold dragons and blue snakes with red tongues around bamboo trees on the seams of his boxing trunks. Good spirits. Scare away demons. Except it didn't work.

When he stayed with his Louisiana Aunt Charley she burned incense. Auntie Charlie gonna take care of her little man. Gonna keep him out of trouble. Nobody gonna hurt him. He was eleven. Then he was a sniper and his fists were bullets. Pumpkins on pavement. Brains in the crosshairs. He sighted down the barrel of an M-14 and bloodied a big Japanese kid in that first fight in Hawaii. He did it to get out of the bush, to win money for the lifers who knew he'd been Golden Gloves; for Mai, who said she'd never leave Vietnam, where her father and his father were buried.

Snow raked the streetlight and wet his hair. His hands went inside his pockets, and then rubbed his face. He wanted to wrap his hands tight, put on the gloves, work a bag at Kronk's until his blood moved. If he could spar—trade some hard time in the ring, he'd get his balance. A match would help, but this round was over.

TKO.

That dancer in the Gold Monkey straddled a tattooed biker, belt chains rubbing her belly, beard like sandpaper against her nipples. She faced him, five dollar bill poking out of her G-string. Her hips pulsed, her hair feathering the biker's face. No. When she moved his hands away, he pushed her between his knees, his fingers around her throat. Yes. He forced a thumb in her mouth. Fucking bitch. That girl was dumped on her ass when Homeboy came out of the dark, landed a left that rocked the biker good. The biker stood, but a right put him down, legs at a funny angle, trickle of blood from his narrow beak and thin lips. The cold wind stirred and felt good on Homeboy's face; it dried the blood on his hands.

Mai loved his face. She traced her fingers down his nose and around his mouth. Beautiful American. Her hair went through his fingers, and he touched the small of her back and felt her breasts against his chest, loving her. Forget the war; he remembered Mai. When they made love, monsoon rain on a tin roof sliding off in sheets, there was only Mai's warm body. He was a soldier. Soldiers were ghosts.

Auntie Charley spoke in a rhythm he didn't understand. Candles burned and he heard wood popping in the stove against a steady bayou rain, the dampness creeping in. On the back porch, sent for an armload of wood, Homebody stared into the rain. The train ride from Detroit to Louisiana had tired him. He missed his father, who was out of work and unable to support a boy who stood in the strange darkness on his Auntie's porch, his skin crawling with gooseflesh. Only temporary, his father said. Homeboy heard alligators slip from the banks—a splash; he smelled air dead with mold. His mind raced at the swamp's edge alive with movement, with sound, and he froze. Auntie Charley was in the doorway. The light behind her hid her face. They only shadows, little man. Can't harm you. The swamp full of life. Listen, you. He listened. That's a bobcat. Rabbit. Owl.

Later that night, head full of sleep, mosquitoes buzzing around the bed covered with netting, he heard his Auntie humming. Through a crack in the door he saw her bathing, naked from the waist up. She leaned before a tub filled with steaming water, washing under her arms, then her breasts, her skin glistening in lantern light. He fell asleep to his Auntie's voice.

Mai was pregnant, asleep, Homeboy's ear pressed against her round belly; insects hummed at the screened window, seeking the electric glow from a small bulb inside the hooch. He'd fight his way out of Vietnam, take Mai with him; he'd win money for the lifers who'd bet against the young Japanese who was very good. But Mai's ancestors were stronger, her dead father reaching from the grave, reminding her she was Vietnamese. And her son's spirit, though half-American, would remain whole in Vietnam. Waking is the dusky morning light, Mai said, You come back, Manny. Live here when the war is over. He'd come back, then Mai would know how much he loved her.

Homeboy slipped into an alley and ran, springing down the pavement on the balls of his feet, his legs loosening with the power he felt coming into them. He shadowboxed, his fists pounding the air at a figure he saw in the dark against falling snow. The Japanese was against the ropes, covering his face with both gloves, a deep cut above his left eye. The bell rang. Homeboy went to his corner; it was the seventh round. He heard his trainer's voice. Take him. The eye. He spit into a cup and planted his feet firmly on the mat. He'd make the Japanese bleed, give the lifers what they wanted. He hit the eye with a succession of hard rights. Again and again. He tasted blood; he drew his opponent's strength out of him and made it his own.

Homeboy slowed, breathing heavily, his lungs on fire with too much oxygen, the way he tired when the Japanese gave him an uppercut that rattled his jaw, then a hook glancing off his temple. He tagged the Japanese with a straight right, and another shot like a bullet sent him to the mat. The referee counted to ten and stopped the fight. It was over.

The Japanese bowed.

The Lifers collected money.

Auntie Charley knew he was strong, put him to work splitting wood; his body hardened. With each blow of the maul, wood split and released a force that grew in his arms, his legs. She fed him cornbread, shrimp Creole, blackened catfish, and it warmed his blood. For three years he worked part time on a shrimp boat, pulled and mended nets. His muscles wrapped taut and lean around him. One day he whipped a large white boy who called him nigger. He was fourteen.

The biker was dead, Mai's gold dragons unable to save Homeboy for what he'd trained his entire life, unable to make something of himself the way his father, dead now for three years, said he would. You're a fighter, Emmanuel. Anyone can see that. He'd connected with the biker, his body and mind working perfectly together, and once set in motion, couldn't be stopped. It was the same in the bush, his face dark with camo, the M-14 resting in his arms and snug into his shoulder, his eye pressed against the scope. An NVA walking on a trail 200 yards away. The distance meant nothing to Homeboy, like the size of the white boy who thought he could beat him. Then he pulled the trigger.

Auntie Charley put her hands on his arms. Too strong, you. Even her magic was powerless against the police from Houma, who came looking for him while he hid in a pirogue in a bayou behind his Auntie's cabin. Later, at the train station, she kissed his cheek. Make Auntie proud. She see you again. The train moved slowly along the tracks. Auntie Charley waved and then disappeared.

Homeboy came out of the alley onto Mack Avenue. A Detroit city bus slowed for its stop, the door opening with a hiss. A woman struggled to collect her belongings. She tugged on a stroller, plastic bags hanging from its handles. She was alone. Snow settled on her hair, the shoulders of her wool coat, the blanket she pulled over a child tucked in her arms. A police cruiser slowed, then it turned around in the alley. "Can I help you, miss?" Homeboy said. The woman averted her eyes, the stroller bumping the bus steps. "Can I help?" he said. The police cruiser turned on its siren. The woman flinched. Then it sped away on Mack Avenue. She was inside the lighted bus. Homeboy stood in bus fumes, put his bloodied hands inside his jacket, and then he walked to his apartment.

Inside, a shaded lamp glowing on the bureau,

Homeboy stared into a mirror reflecting his boxing trophies, the embroidered trunks, the robe hanging on a hook—Homeboy, framed by dragons and snakes, stenciled clearly on the back. He saw his reflection, his small eyes straining to see something far away—Mai, and the child he'd never know.

SNAKES AND DRAGONS

If you ask me what I remember, I will tell you this:

I was a boy in Vietnam. My name is Tim Tran. The place of my employment, Detroit Linen and Uniform Service, is where they call me "Little Buddy." I do not like the name, but what does it matter? It is only a name. My real name is Tran Danh Thu. My father called me T.T. My mother gave me this name because she said Thu means autumn in Vietnamese, and a Vietnam autumn, when the rains come, washes everything clean. "It is a new beginning, Thu," my mother told me. "Each time you are reborn."

My mother was a poor woman, never married. She did laundry for North Vietnamese soldiers after they liberated Saigon. Today it is called Ho Chi Minh City, and that is where she died with cancer in her lungs. Her name was Mai. I think about my mother each day as I load dirty hospital and hotel linen onto a conveyor belt and dump it into giant sterilization vats. I set the locks. All computerized now. I do not think about filth and disease. I watch steam rise to fluorescent lights. It remind me of Vietnam when sweat runs down my body inside my Detroit Linen Service uniform. I look good in the uniform, I think. The sun in Detroit, during late July, hides behind skyscrapers, and rain drops linger in the air, but I cannot see them. They call this humidity. Water in the air.

The Americans, mostly blacks, do not like the job; they say it is an immigrant's job; they say for people with last names like Lopez, Garcia, and Ramirez; they call them spics. The spics call them niggers. I do not like this name-calling; I do not like the jokes. The few whites working at Detroit Linen and Uniform Service drive the big, white trucks. "Little Buddy," the whites say, "you got that laundry ready for the Skipper?" Then they laugh. I do not understand the reference, though I know it is from an old TV program, and I laugh too; I try to fit in.

Since I am thirty-two years and still a bachelor, I change clothes in the locker room and leave work; I go to a strip club called the Gold Monkey on Mack Avenue; it is the oldest in Detroit. I go there because my father talked about it, about the beautiful women; but what I see are clownish, half-naked women dancing around a smudged pole. They do not show us their real faces. I go there because I am waiting for a sign. I give money to the women; slip a dollar bill here and a dollar bill there into their underwear. They dance in front of me for a while and then move to another table, where other men wait with fistfuls of dollar bills. I do not drink much beer because it cost eight dollar. The rock and roll music reminds me of my father, reminds me my father was black. I listen to the music and think about why the Americans abandoned us in South Vietnam and took my father with them. What choice did he have? For almost two years we were a family. My mother had told me this, said he was a soldier stationed at Camp Sally near Phu Bai. She told me he was a professional boxer, and called away to box in places like Thailand and Japan. The commanders bet money on him and won. Maybe this is why I like to gamble. When I ask my mother to tell me more, she refuses, says, "Forget about him. He is a ghost." But I somehow knew he chose to fight with his fists so he did not have to kill Vietnamese people.

"Why a ghost?" I once ask my mother.

"Bring in the wood," she say, "build a fire."

Because I am *bui dai*, a child of dust, I was invisible, and different from other children. Yet I knew there is I separate from We. I do not mind it now, but as a child they called me names. The other children said my nose was too broad and flat, my skin too dark, not a pretty yellow like theirs; they said I looked like an animal, a monkey. They said my spirit would not find rest. In Vietnam there are monkey bridges made of bamboo the people cross single file; I am crossing a bridge, too, alone, but it is in my mind, and you cannot see it. My mother said children were cruel, to pay them no attention. "Ignore them," she said. "Tomorrow you will be different than you are today."

If I stare long enough at the darkened stage, lights spinning blue and green, the room becomes liquid with my father walking toward me. He is wearing boxing trunks embroidered with snakes and dragons; his eyes look into mine, but I am not an opponent; I am not the enemy. He is a black man with strong arms and legs, a powerful chest. I feel his warm palms against my small hands; I am a child he scoops up and holds; I smell sea salt, the South China Sea, and his sweat from hitting a bag hung on the branch of a jambu tree. He is a good smell. I burrow my head into his chest. This is my father; he will protect me. He floats in the room, magically appears here and there in flashing strobe lights; it's as if I am dancing with my father, but then he lets me go and I'm lost in gun fire pounding from speakers. My father is a strong man, but he cannot hold me; for a moment I am afraid until I hear my father's voice: "Don't worry little T. T. I will teach you to box. Your mother will sew dragons and snakes on your robe." Somewhere in my peripheral vision, I see my mother nodding. "Learn to defend," my father says. His eyes are darker than betel nut. I stare back. "Yes, father. I will," I say.

POINT MAN

I suppose the real reason I left for Gabriel's after arguing with Jean was I knew Randy Kodoski would be in the bar, like always, and I needed a drink. Jean didn't want me to go out, made a big fuss about it, said I was going to end up a drunk like Kodoski if I wasn't careful. They'd been together for a time before I came home from Vietnam. I never thought much about them because that's the kind of thing that'll make you crazy . . . make you say and do things you'll later regret. It might not hit you until you're down the road a year or two, but sooner or later, when you least expect it, a feeling from deep in your gut will have its say, get right in your face, make a fool out of you.

After that night, north of the suburbs where I'd been with Kodoski and Kasia, I was surprised to find a note from Jean on the refrigerator door:

Micky, I know you'll understand because
I'm just like you. Love, Jean.

That was it.

Thinking we all had to make it in this world any way we could, I ripped the note into little pieces, tossed it into the kitchen trash. Wondering where your life was going to take you, like I kept telling Jean, wouldn't make your life any easier. You had to take care of business, do whatever was necessary to keep going.

That's what my old man taught me, how to take care of business, which he did up until he died after I'd come home from my tour. He worked for thirty years on the Chrysler assembly line, and eight weeks after he spot-welded his last fender onto a '70 New Yorker he had a heart attack at the dinner table. His face was already a shade of gray by the time two EMS attendants wheeled him into the ambulance. I'd seen that look in Nam so I knew he wouldn't last long. His dying scared me, not because I was afraid of death, but because I didn't feel a thing. It wasn't until later, years later, like most everything that happened did I realize I didn't have a father anymore. He was gone for good. I guess that's why I'm thinking about the night Jean left and didn't come back.

That night when I finally closed the apartment door and backed out into the hallway, Jean glared at me like someone ready for a fight. I heard the lock turn, the security chain slide into place. I heard Jean cry.

On the street I looked at my watch; it was midnight. Plenty of time to have a drink with Kodoski, I thought. When I got into the Mercury, where it had been parked on Gray Street, I took a bottle of whiskey from the glove compartment, had a good swallow, and felt my throat go numb. After another good hit on the bottle I lit a cigarette, looked into the rearview mirror at my eyes. Even then I liked it when the whiskey leveled out in my brain. The whiskey plateau.

The Merc came to life with a roar. I rolled the windows down, felt the engine's power under my foot, and a breeze like hot breath coming into the car. It was good to be out of the apartment. I felt like a bird that found its way out of a chimney, flying blind over houses and trees.

The traffic on the Edsel Ford Expressway was heavy, the air coming in dry as dust. I changed lanes and took an exit ramp up to Chalmers Avenue. At the next green light I turned a corner and drove past the abandoned Conner Park Projects. The buildings looked like the ones I'd seen in Hue after Tet.

I was anxious to get to the bar so I hit the gas.

After a few more blocks, I pulled into the parking lot behind Gabriel's, and slid the Merc in next to Kodoski's truck. My T-shirt was soaked. I had a short-sleeved shirt in the back seat so I put it on. The parking lot was empty, but I looked around before getting out of the car and going into the bar. Several people turned to look at me when I opened the door. Two guys were standing next to a pool table under the light overhead. I heard a sharp crack, a ball drop, and "You don't know shit, Mr. Brown," one said to the other above the swearing and laughter mixed in with rock and roll coming from the jukebox. At first I didn't see Kodoski, and thought about leaving, and then I spotted him at the end of the bar. He wore a fatigue jacket which I thought was odd, it being so hot and all. I took a stool next to him, put my hand on his left shoulder where half his jacket sleeve was pinned. "Not too shabby," I said, and pointed to the barmaid who was drinking at the other end of the bar, something clear, vodka or gin. Her laugh exposed her bucked teeth, her lips were turned up in a pout under a small rounded nose, almost rodent-like in a cute sort of way.

Kodoski leaned over, slid a quarter off the bar. "She's new," he said. "Her name's Kasia. C'mon, I'll flip you for her." Kasia watched us, and then came down to our end of the bar; she stood in front of Kodoski, wiped her hands on a towel. "We don't allow no gambling in here," she said.

Kodoski smiled. "We're not gambling. Ever since Nam I haven't been able to tell my head from my tail." He had his hand over the quarter. The pool sharks argued about whose quarter was up for the next game.

"Are you one of them Vietnam vets?" she asked, looking at me.

I shrugged, thinking about the bad time Kodoski had gone through on Firebase Henderson. That was in Nam during monsoon. After the attack, we found NVA skeletons lying in craters left by mortar rounds exploding all over the red clay hilltop; it was a mass grave no one knew was there. When Doc Crowe stumbled onto Kodoski under tent posts, rib cages and skulls, he was knocked out, covered in mud and rats the medics had to chase off so they could pump him full of morphine. He was dusted-off in a chopper that same night, taken to a hospital ship anchored in Cam Rahn Bay. I didn't see him until we were back in Detroit.

"He don't talk much," Kasia said, then walked away to wait on a woman who'd had too much to drink, who wore too much make-up to cover the miles, her clownish face a smear of ruby lips, dark rouge, and deep lavender eye shadow. She tried to talk, tried to say something, but it all came out in a slur. "I'd never let my daughter come into a dump like this," she said. "It ain't a place for no lady." Then she lit a smoke, looked at the ceiling, waited for an answer.

Once Kasia was out of earshot, Kodoski said, "I've got something." He pulled his fatigue jacket up to show me a .45 automatic, its barrel tucked into his pants.

I looked around the bar. "Are you crazy?" I said.

"Some rats are going to die at the spillway tonight."

"I didn't plan on this," I told him.

"We're not robbing a fucking bank for Chrissakes. Just a little hunting is all."

It was closing when Kodoski asked Kasia for another drink, but he wanted her to have one with him, leave the bar, go someplace quiet. "Don't worry," he said, seeing the look on her face. "He can't get it up," then motioned to me. "Nothing to be afraid of."

"Looks healthy to me," Kasia said. I was glad she had a sense of humor. I thought everything might turn out all right in spite of the lousy feeling I had after the fight with Jean.

I heard the walk-in cooler door go thunk. Kasia came out with a six pack of beer in a grocery sack. "Take this," she said, "and wait for me outside. I'll be out in a minute."

Kodoski nudged me and we left the bar. Outside, I felt tar sticking to the bottoms of my tennis shoes as I walked across the parking lot to get the whiskey from the Merc. "She's not coming," I said after a while, and gave Kodoski the bottle. "She'll be out," he said.

Kodoski's appeal to women, the way he had with them, amazed me. I wondered what it had been like for him and Jean, wondered what it was she'd been attracted to. He knew how to talk to women, seemed to know when he had the edge, when he was about to get in. He bragged about getting laid as if he'd solved some problem, explained the process as if he knew everything there was to know about fucking, as if there was anything to know. The women were just curious, I think. Maybe they wondered what it would be like to ball a guy with one arm. But he made them laugh, and they actually seemed to like him until they figured out he was mostly a fake, and wouldn't stay with them for more than a few days, weeks, or at the most, a month or two.

"How's Jean," Kodoski asked.

"Fine," I lied. We never talked about Jean, not

in a way I thought settled anything. I wanted to tell him about the look on Jean's face when I'd gone out the door, but decided against it.

Jean never said where she'd been, except to say out with her girlfriends. It bothered me. They'd go somewhere a few times a week, on Saturdays when they worked the late shift at Polanski's Vegetable Warehouse over on Mack Avenue. At first I didn't think about it much, but her boss, this fat Polack name Louie Polanski, made time with all the girls who worked there, married or not. He invited them into the back room to show them the biggest cucumber he said they'd ever see. Jean told me all about it. I was worried, accused her of partying with Polanski when she wouldn't tell me where she went with her friends. When I asked her to quit her job, she said, "You are such an asshole. I thought you had more class."

"Asshole?" I said. "The asshole is that disgusting vegetable Polack."

"Okay, Mickiewicz," she said. "I get it. Double standards."

I told her I didn't hate anybody who didn't deserve it.

The Clinton River spillway drains into Lake St.

Clair about fifteen miles outside Detroit. I'd gone out there with Kodoski when we were kids. All night we fished, kept a fire burning near the river until the sun came up, watched it rise over cattails and reeds in the shallows near the river's mouth; at dawn the sky was burnt orange, the same sky over Firebase Henderson when Kodoski got hit.

"Don't look so glum, hero." She was standing near the door of the truck. I smelled her. Stale booze and cigarettes. I got out and let Kasia slide across the seat. She'd changed into a skirt, and it rode up her thigh, showed her pale legs where they rubbed against the shifter.

Kodoski started the truck, put it into gear, his hand brushing her legs. "Your legs remind me of Grand Boulevard," he said.

Kasia cocked her head. "How's that?"

"They go all the way to Joy Road," Kodoski said, then laughed at his own joke.

We left the parking lot where a few noisy stragglers had come out of the bar to find their cars. Once on Jefferson Avenue we drove north, passed the Old Grosse Point mansions, the yacht club, and followed the Detroit River shoreline to Lake St. Clair until we came to the Clinton River. Kodoski turned onto a two-track road paralleling the river; he steered over potholes and ruts, down shifted.

Finally we stopped, and Kodoski killed the engine.

The spillway was different, not at all like it was when we were kids. In front of us was a '57 Chevy full of bullet holes, its sharp chromed fins visible in the headlights. Behind the Chevy was a mountain of trash: rusted bed springs, dirty mattresses, pieces of twisted steel, fifty-five-gallon drums, cans, tires, you name it.

A hot wind blew in from across the lake. Some rain clouds moved in. The spillway was lit in moonlight. The water seemed like a sheet of aluminum foil. Far off a roll of thunder. Kodoski jumped out of the truck, the headlights still shining on the junk pile. "Did you see that?" he said, then pulled the automatic from his belt, pointing to a spot near a charred, smoking tire. The truck's engine cooled, ticked in the night air.

"See what?" Kasia said.

"There!" shouted Kodoski. He waved the pistol at one target, then another. "A fucking rat!" He fired.

When the echo died in the canal, Kasia climbed out of the truck. "Looked more like a cat." Her voice was calm, collected. It was not what I expected from her, especially since she stood between two strangers, between one shooting imaginary rats, and the other feeling nervous as a cherry walking point. I didn't know whether she was brave or stupid, the two traits being so close together if you think about it.

"I know what a rat looks like," Kodoski said. He waved the gun around. "Missed that son-of-a-bitch, too. What we need is a goddamn dog. You want to be my dog?"

"Woof," Kasia said. "Give the gun to our hero. Let's you and me take a stroll." Kodoski slapped the grip into my palm as if he were handing off a baton. "Don't hurt yourself," he said.

I turned off the headlights, sat in the driver's seat, and smoked a cigarette, examined the automatic. After moving concrete all day the gun was light, hardly noticeable except for its warm feel in the palm of my hand.

Jean never liked the guys I worked with, didn't trust them, didn't like the fact I'd sometimes stop at Gabriel's to have a few drinks and shoot a few games of pool with them. Even though I looked forward to working for the Giovanni brothers about as much as I looked forward to the headaches I'd get some mornings pressing down on me, I crawled out of bed, and drove to Eight Mile Road and Gratiot Avenue at seven a.m. to pick up drunks and welfare bums waiting on the corner for a day job. I never thought of them as bad men, not in the sense they'd hurt anyone. They were no worse than some of the guys I knew in Nam. But Jean wouldn't have anything to do with them. She thought they were the same ones we saw every night on the eleven o'clock news, schmucks caught in a gangland crossfire or a liquor store hold up. Maybe they were.

I got out of the truck and walked over to the smoking trash heap where it seemed to move in the dark, dotted with glowing embers. I pulled out a coffee can wedged in between a tire and some old bed springs. The can was warm; it still had its plastic lid. I walked over to the water's edge, threw the can into the spillway where its bottom turned up to shine in the moonlight. I heard Kasia laugh, Kodoski's muffled voice in the darkness behind me.

Taking aim, I shot three times. Each time a cartridge ejected from the .45 I felt the recoil radiate up my arm, into my elbow and shoulder; each time a silver spray hung over the spillway, then the coffee can sank before I could get off another shot. It felt right because I was always a damn good shot, hardly ever missed, and it was okay knowing there was still something I could do the way it was supposed to be done.

In those days I wanted Jean to appreciate me because I worked hard to keep us going, tried to save some money to move out to the suburbs where she thought it was safe. She stayed with me in the Gray Street Apartments for three years, on the east side, near Jefferson Avenue, not far from the Chrysler Assembly Plant and the Detroit River. When it's clear, which it hardly ever is, I can still see across the roofs of other houses, watch lake freighters go up and down the river.

At first, Jean was pretty excited about the apartment, the hardwood floors, tall windows in the living room, a fireplace that didn't work because the chimney wasn't safe. But more than anything she hated coming home after dark. There were only a few worn locks anybody could open if they wanted to. When we first moved in, though, I felt good about the place because I'd started to work steady. After we hauled all our stuff upstairs, and Jean arranged everything the way she wanted, we'd watch the river freeze, then in the spring we saw the ice break up, the ore boats begin to move slow through the channel.

At the spillway, a quarter mile downriver, a car passed over the Jefferson bridge. A few lights were on in the new condominiums near the river's mouth, and a freighter beyond inching upriver. I thought someone might've heard the shots. I got nervous thinking they'd call the police, but it was quiet except for the hum of an outboard motor somewhere out on the lake.

I walked back to the truck, dropped the tailgate, let the clip slip out of the automatic. There were two cartridges left. One in the clip and one in the chamber. I sat on the tailgate, put the clip back in and made sure the safety was on when I saw Kasia and Kodoski coming. She looked ruffled; her hair was matted in sweat against her forehead. "Did you get off on that gun?" she asked.

"Sure he did," Kodoski intruded. "He's Point-man, the killer—that's what we called him in Nam."

I didn't like it when Kodoski talked about Vietnam; it made me think of guys in our squad—Pineapple, Hippie, Tennessee; it didn't matter what anybody called you because you were in a fantasy world that didn't matter. One day you were joking and getting stoned with your pals; the next, you were calling in a medevac, and you never saw them again. Like Bobby Strong, a skinny black kid from Chicago, a cherry we called Face because his was unusual: pock marks, deep set eyes, thick lips stretched across a wide set of teeth in a mouth with more teeth than a mouth has.

One night Kodoski told Face he was the horniest bastard he'd ever known, said Face would fuck a snake if he could get someone to hold the head. We all laughed, even Face. The next day on point Face set off a tripwire rigged to a Claymore mine the gooks probably took off some dead grunt. It blew his arm and leg off. Before the dust settled, Face was on a chopper headed for a Da Nang hospital. He might be wheeling around Chicago right now.

"Here," Kasia said. "This will cool you down." A bottle of beer fizzed in my hand.

Kodoski set his beer on the tailgate, picked up the .45, and said, "You know, people are a lot like animals. . . ."

"You're stoned," Kasia said, unbuttoning his shirt, running her hand inside.

"I'm telling you," Kodoski said. "we're all animals. Right Pointman?" Then he put his arm around Kasia, the muzzle of the .45 pointed at her back. Slowly, moving out of Kodoski's grasp, she began to undress, unzipped her skirt, let her blouse slip off her shoulders until most of her clothes were around her ankles. She stepped out of them, left them in a heap in the dirt.

I slid out of my own clothes one morning after drinking all night at Gabriel's, and got into bed with Jean, trying to be quiet. For a while I listened to a fan running on top of the dresser; it squeaked and hummed, vibrated as it rotated back and forth circulating a room full of humid air. I heard a siren not far away, voices in the alley, the city getting louder. I couldn't sleep so I turned on a light next to the bed. Jean sighed and rolled over. The light made her squint. "It's early," she said. "When did you come in?"

"Just a few minutes ago. Couldn't sleep."

Jean sat up and stroked the back of my neck. "Where were you, Micky? I was worried."

I let my head lean against Jean's hand; her hand felt good on the back of my neck. Then she got on top of me. I put my hands on her hips. "I've got to get ready for work," I said.

"Take a day off."

"I can't, Jean. You know that." I rolled her off to one side. In the shower I wondered how much money it was going to take to move out to the suburbs, how much it would take to raise kids where Jean wanted.

"I want to be an otter," Kasia said, "and swim in the river." She turned and ran toward the water. We followed her down the embankment. When she got to a concrete retaining wall, her bra came off. She climbed down a ladder built into the wall, and quickly disappeared from sight.

Kodoski set the gun down on the ledge and took off his clothes. I wondered if he was right about people and animals. When I eased into the water, I noticed the current didn't pull much in the river where it flattened out the way it did close to the mouth. I watched Kodoski float on his back as he drifted in and out of light coming and going behind the clouds. Kasia dog-paddled towards me. Her forehead made a V through the water, her slicked-back hair tucked tightly behind her ears. I tried to float, but booze pounded in my head. The air felt thick and still. Kasia came up against me then, her small breasts pushed into me, drops of water slid down her face. I held her for a minute, tried to kiss her, but she went under the water, breaking the grasp of my arms around her neck, laughing when she came up for air a few feet away.

Thinking it was too late to go home; too late to make things right with Jean, I swam back to the wall and climbed out of the spillway. I reached for my pants, stubbing the .45 with my toe, catching it just before it fell into the water.

The gun was still warm when I picked it up, pointed it at the water, watched Kodoski swim towards me. His face was pale in the moonlight, all the blood gone out of it as he struggled to make the last few yards. Kasia trailed behind. I looked down the barrel, caught the moon reflected on the water, sighted down the barrel at a shiny, bloodless face.

"You know that feeling, Mick," I heard Kodoski shout, "the one at the end of a high? You think you're supposed to take care of some unfinished business, but you never know what it is."

"Yeah," I said, "I've noticed it." I wanted to throw the gun over their heads, hear it splash in the water behind them, but I couldn't let go of it.

Kasia came out of the spillway, shivered in the morning air, water glistening on her stomach. I put Kodoski's field jacket around her shoulders. She held it tight against herself. And just as Kodoski climbed out of the spillway some rain clouds let loose. Big plops fell around us as we walked up the embankment toward the truck. Half dressed, we stood there a minute, all of us, I guess, wishing we were home in our beds.

When I parked the Merc in front of the Gray Street Apartments it was still raining. I stood on the sidewalk for a minute, letting the rain soak me. A cool breeze blew in from downriver. I felt it coming from places I'd never been, would probably never go. The wind whistled through broken windows of abandoned buildings and decayed warehouses near the river. I listened for a while; then I went up to the apartment and found the door unchained, unlocked, Jean's closet empty of clothes.

WHEN WATER BREAKS FROM THE SHORE

You can't sleep with your best friend's wife and
not feel anything, even when his wife's left him,
and she wants to sleep with you. You can't, but you
do. You know there's no wisdom in this. At Gabe's
Bar, Mick says, "Let's go up north." You never lived
up north, owned a dog or a gun, but you do now.
You keep a .45 in the glove box, and when you
leave the bar, Detroit's a shadow skirting the edges
of pavement and chrome.

"Where's the wisdom?" you ask your friend.

"Piss on wisdom," he says, because he's drunk,
and it's been one of those nights when the beers
go down like angel pee, and you're both twenty-
three and you're home two years from the war.

Michigan Highway 25 ribbons in the headlights.
Snowflakes come at the windshield like tiny meteors.
You're driving Mick's Mercury, steering it with one
hand because it's all you have, because Mick's obsessed
with Jean, and he can't see past the car's windows.

One night Jean cleans out her closet on Gray Street, and shows at your door an hour later. You're glad to see her; glad she's holding a six pack in one hand, keys to your car in the other. Mick doesn't know you've already told her you love the curve of her back, the slope of it disappearing under a sheet, the way she sits on the edge of your bed to comb her hair. You've told her you love her.

"What's in here?" Mick says, rifling through the glove box, pushing aside the automatic. "Bingo," he says, and lights a joint you know you'll need to stay awake long enough to buy more beer from a cooler where night crawlers and red worms are sold at the Bay Port Store. You'll need more beer to stop thinking about Jean and Hawaii, where you met Mick on R and R, and Jean was there, too, but you knew she would be, and now you can't remember if you went there to see your best friend and his future wife because you were too scared to lose your virginity in Thailand, or if you were already in love with Jean. You were nineteen.

Your arm on the steering wheel feels like wood. Fields slide past in red taillights fading into a rear view winter, and you're thinking about when Jean asks you if Mick talks about her. You tell her no. Behind you the snow is sand white like frost on a window pane you and Jean watch break loose

from its own shoreline and melt down the glass.
You wanted her to stay in Hawaii so you could lose
yourself in her body. You almost said you loved her,
but Mick's voice is like machinery, like an assembly line at Ford's, saying he'll go A-W-O-L to be
with the people he loves. You feel ocean spray kiss
your face and thirsty palms bend to drink words
you've lost in a photograph you've kept now for
three years—a photograph of Jean walking away,
down the beach, bikini clad and two dimensional.

"Daylight," you say, and point to patches of
snow turned burnt orange at the edge of sky and
ice on Saginaw Bay. Mick says, "Turn here," and
takes the .45 from the glove box. He shoves it inside his coat. You're wishing you had two arms
instead of one because if you have to pull Mick
through a hole in the ice, you will, even if you
both drown.

"Slow down," Mick says, and points to a place
on the shore that's a frozen boat ramp. You are the
ice. There's white all around except for a black dot
three hundred yards from shore. He opens the car
door; you see ice sliding past, as if the car stands
still, as if the lake is a greased ball bearing spinning
underneath the car—shiny and silver like stainless
steel. You want to say, "Get back in the car," but
you watch Mick plant his feet on the ice, hang

onto the door while you turn the wheel. The car spins faster, and Mick drifts out and back like a water skier behind a boat. The soles of his street shoes skid across the ice.

When you were kids you wanted Mick to skate on a city pond, but Mick said he needed to eat, so you followed him into Club Eleven. His mother's there with a woman she calls Aunt Peggy. The smoke burns your eyes. Her face is painted around two dark spots set back in her skull. "Ma," Mick said, "Ma." Three dollars pushed through a puddle on the bar. Bills folded wet in Mick's hand.

Mick laughs, pulls himself into the car, and says, "Right there."

It's dawn. A fog lifts off the ice. You can't see the shore; you can't locate yourself. Mick stands at the ice shanty, pulling on a Master Lock, but the door doesn't budge. You wonder if Mick's bothered to change the locks to his apartment like he said he would one night at Gabe's Bar; he's not going to let that bitch back into his life for one minute, he's said. By the time you're ready to leave Gabe's he's said he loves her.

You make love to Jean, and she tells you Mick's life is hard. You're holding Jean with your good arm; you hold her while the phantom arm slips through her and disappears like she will when she decides she's going back to Mick. But you hold her.

"There's a whole world under the ice," Mick says, and shoots off the lock. The sound carries across the frozen lake. A crack starts. "Holy Mother," Mick says. The ice doesn't part; you're not swept out to Lake Huron. You don't drown. Mick goes into the ice shanty, and you both stare into a hole; you can see the bottom, ripples of sand; you both wait and watch.

ANIMOOSH

County Road 550 was slippery, a heavy mist getting slick on the blacktop to Big Bay, when Ray Halliday and three other men and the dog, Animoosh, little dog in Ojibwa, passed a sign that said, *Slippery When Wet.* The Dead River, the *River Des Morts*, Earl called it each time they crossed the bridge, flowed from Tourist Lake, and over an old hydroelectric dam. The black water picked up volume as it cascaded over boulders and gravel riffles. Ray stood at the river's edge and saw the water glisten and sparkle in the moonlight. For a hundred yards downriver fires dotted both banks. There were dancing flames and figures, shadows drinking beer and passing whiskey bottles to ward off the cold. Every fifteen minutes or so someone shouted, "They're running!" and people grabbed their waders and nets. The heartier ones splashed into the water without boots, and then everyone laughed because there weren't any fish—they weren't running.

This called for more firewood, more beer and whiskey, more dancing to songs people sang from memory and ones they made up. Ray heard Earl's voice boom downriver. He sang an Irish drinking song:

Now everybody's died, so until our tears are dried.
We'll drink and drink and drink and drink,
and then we'll drink some more.
We'll dance and sing and fight until the early
morn,
and then throw up, pass out, wake up
and then we'll drink some more!

Drift, Ray's friend since grade school, handed Robby a fifth of Jim Beam, and Robby took a long swig. "You're getting the hang of her now," Drift said. Robby was new in town. He was from Florida. Ray noticed something familiar about him, told him he'd been there himself, but didn't tell Robby he was once married to a woman he met in Key West named Cheryl. Ray didn't share many details about his personal life, figured once he opened himself up it would lead to having to explain himself, and Ray didn't like going too deep into himself. It was uncomfortable and

Cheryl was twenty years ago. All he remembered was that she seemed more in love with a dead guy's photo than she was with him. He didn't like being jealous over a ghost. It didn't make sense. So one day he packed a duffle, stopped at Sloppy Joe's for a drink and then boarded a bus for Michigan. Out of all his moves, it wasn't his finest.

When Robby came into Remie's Tavern, Ray watched him beat the pants off everyone shooting pool, but he was smart enough to buy drinks with the money he won. He was the best pool shot Ray had ever seen, and buying drinks was a good way to make friends. Since he had no where stay, Ray directed him to the Hotel Janzen and introduced him to his girlfriend, Jeanie, who had her own room down the hall from Ray. Like everyone in the Janzen, Jeanie was down on her luck, but she was resourceful and Ray thought the kid might have reminded her of a son she'd lost but didn't want to talk about; in a few days Jeanie found Robby a bed, a couple of chairs and a small table. The kid was grateful. They got the stuff moved and the next night Ray invited him to go fishing.

"What do you do with them all?" Robby said.

"Cook some," Drift said. "Take 'em up to Big Bay. Give some to Earl. He sells 'em in his bar. Uses 'em for bait."

ANIMOOSH

In the darkness, Ray watched Drift and Robby. Though they hadn't said much to each other on the way to Big Bay, Robby acted as if he might like Drift, but everyone liked Drift. Mostly they felt superior to him. What you didn't like about yourself was what you found wrong with other people, Ray thought. If you felt superior to certain people then you made fun of people like Drift. If you were cheap, you'd blame someone else for scrimping on a tip. If you thought a person was plotting against you, chances were you were scheming just like them.

Then a fisherman threw kerosene on a fire and it scorched the branches of a low hanging red pine and lit the surrounding darkness. A memory of Vietnam came to Ray as they often did. They came in images; they came in odors; they came in sounds. Nam was more than twenty-five years ago, and nobody wanted to hear about it, and Ray accepted that. He'd gotten over that in the first two or three years home from the war, when he was angry, when he'd gotten into bar fights with people who talked like they knew something about it. It didn't matter to Ray if they were for or against the war. He just couldn't take listening to someone who hadn't been there. They didn't belong to the same fraternity, the one that had taken his youth and made him bitter before he was old enough to legally drink.

He'd been on Firebase Henderson two weeks after the North Vietnamese Army attacked and killed seventeen ARVN and U.S. Marines. It was a spooky place and one night while he looked out of a perimeter bunker at shadowy Central Highland Mountains, he asked Homeboy, a kid from Detroit's Eastside, if he'd ever gone smelting. Homeboy told a story about a big catfish his grandfather had caught on the Missouri River. "Big as a man. That's no lie, Ray."

They'd been passing a joint. Homeboy discharged the shells from his shotgun and Ray took the barrel end into his mouth. Homeboy blew smoke into the loading chamber, and Ray inhaled until he couldn't take anymore; he fell backwards against the hard-packed sand bags. "Whoa," Ray said. "That's some shit!"

"Smelt shit," Homeboy said.

They tried to stifle their laughter, but it was impossible; they were too stoned. Far off, ten or fifteen klicks, Ray and Homeboy saw Cobra gunships firing on a ridgeline, the undulation of tracer rounds like red blips on a heart monitor. As long as the line on the heart monitor didn't go flat, they'd be okay. Then it got quiet. "I don't want to kill nobody," Homeboy said, ". . . and that's why I quit the snipers. Got me a nice mama-san in Saigon. Ray nodded.

Lieutenant Harness's big white head appeared in the bunker entrance. "You don't shut the fuck up you're going to get your asses shot off."

"Yes, sir," they said. When Harness was out of sight, Homeboy said, "Smelt sheeeet," and they started up all over again.

Someone downriver yelled, "They're running!" This time they were. Drift tossed Robby a pair of waders, handed him a net, and said, "Have at it, kid."

"What do I do?" Robby said.

"Catch some fish," Ray said, holding onto a five gallon bucket ready to collect whatever smelt Robby might scoop from the Dead.

Robby struggled into the waders and stepped into the swift current. He was tipsy from the whiskey, and it wouldn't be a good idea to lose him his first week in town; he didn't want the kid to get a bad impression of the Upper Peninsula.

Where was Animoosh? "Animoosh!" Ray yelled. Then he saw Moosher near the river, not far from the kid. "Robby!" Ray shouted. Robby turned to see Moosher following him to the next boulder. And just as Robby made it, the dog jumped and Ray saw Moosher's claws slide down a moss covered rock. "Goddamn," Ray said. The dog swirled in an eddy near the shore; twice he went round and round. "Drift! Grab Moosher!"

Drift was close enough, but when he reached for the dog, it was swept from the whirlpool, and headed downstream like an adrenaline freak in a kayak. Ray ran down the riverbank, keeping his eye on the dog, whose head was above water, but then was lost in the foam as the river funneled through a narrow spot and around rocks. Ray heard Earl and his crowd singing. "Hey!" Ray shouted. "Earl!"

Earl turned to look at Ray and saw him pointing at the river. Ray yelled, "My dog! He's in the Dead!"

Earl's whisky bottle exploded in flames when he threw it into the fire. A flame shot upward into the night sky. Pine trees hung low and shadowy at the river's edge. A great roar came up from the crowd.

"Hooray!" they shouted.

"It's the bloody apocalypse!" someone else yelled.

"There he goes!" someone said.

"He's out there!" Ray pointed at a patch of white fur on the dog's head visible in the black water.

"Animoosh! Animoosh!" the crowd chanted.

"There he is!" He was moving fast down river and Ray was sure the dog would drown.

Several people ran with their nets to snag the dog. Two people made a swipe and missed. A third almost got him with a bucket tied to a rope. The dog's head went under once. Twice. Earl, who'd been running down the bank, following the dog, jumped in where the river funneled between two big boulders.

"Get him there, between those two rocks," Ray yelled.

Earl jumped into the river, pinned himself against the rocks; the current wanted them, but Earl was strong and grabbed the dog by the scruff of his neck. With one arm the size of a two pound coffee can, he threw Animoosh twenty feet toward shore. Animoosh landed next to a fire pit. Earl had saved his dog.

The crowd cheered. A drunk nobody knew danced around the fire, his arms flailing like a helicopter. The drunk took off his coat and wrapped it around Animoosh. "You're safe with old Chudy, you are, dog," the drunk said, as he cradled Moosher in his arms and let him lap beer from a can of Blatz.

Earl, soaking wet, got close to the fire. Steam came off his clothes. He said, "It's time to wrap it up." Robby still worked the net upstream through the current, dumping thirty or forty smelt at a time into buckets.

Ray said, "Go get those big trash bags outta Earl's truck, Drift."

"What for?"

"You blind? Look at the kid's net. He's killing them out there. And double them."

Earl walked over to the crew. He shivered and his teeth chattered. He said, "I'm going to start the truck." Then he walked up the hill where everyone could see his naked moon ass as he changed out of his wet clothes. Robby dipped again and again and soon there were three forty-gallon plastic trash bags filled to capacity.

"Better triple those bags," Ray said.

"They'll be all right. I doubled them," Drift said.

"Suit yourself," Ray said.

Robby got back to shore and helped Drift carry the bags up to the truck. He held the bottoms so they wouldn't split. When they put them into the back of Earl's truck, Earl said, "Gotta be more than two hundred pounds of fish, and you're gonna clean em, Drift."

"I ain't cleaning all of em," Drift said. He loved smelt, and pound for pound he could eat more than anyone. "Robby'll help, won't you, buddy?" he said.

Robby said, "Never cleaned a fish in my life."

"Ya just cut their heads off with a pair of scissors and pull the guts loose. Leave the tail. Real good eating. Right, Earl?"

"I'll end up cooking most of the damn things, too," Earl said. "Why don't we just put them in my garden?"

"No way," Drift said.

Robby weaved from foot to foot and slurred his words, "How about a big pile of Frense flies?"

"Let's just get the hell up to Big Bay," said Earl.

"I clean em. You cook em." Drift said.

Packed in between three bags of smelt, Drift got up close to the cab in the bed of the truck to get out of the wind. The dog was on the floor between Ray's feet, the heater blowing his wet dog smell filled the cab. Robby complained about the dog, but Animoosh had had a rough night, and it was still twenty minutes to Big Bay. Earl knew the curves in the road and he could shave off a few minutes by taking a short cut through the woods. He'd have to backtrack and weave around and through several vehicles parked close to the river. He knew a way out, he said, but it would take them back towards town a half mile or so and then they'd be able to get back on Co. Rd. 550, cross the Dead River Bridge again and head up the highway to Big Bay.

It was slow going among the tall red pines. Drift sat cushioned by the smelt bags. Robby was green around the gills.

Earl said, "That dog's busy in the head." But there were times when Animoosh appeared to have had a lobotomy. Ray had to stand next to his food and say, "Eat your food, Moosher. Go ahead. Eat it, Moosher." The dog would bark and look at Ray, grab a toy, lay it next to his food dish, then bark some more before he'd finally finish what was left in his bowl.

Robby said, "That dog's retarded." But Animoosh was a self-regulator, didn't gobble food like it was his sole mission in life. Too bad more people weren't like Animoosh. There were some who didn't know when to quit. They took and took. A lot of them Ray wouldn't call busy in the head, either, like his ex-wife. Ray tried hard not to have bad feelings about his Florida experience, but the woman he'd married was obsessed with a dead boyfriend who had been a Navy fighter pilot; Ray never quite believed the details that changed with each telling. He had drowned in the South China Sea; his body had washed ashore in Da Nang; he had been attacked by a shark; both his legs were broken when he ejected from his F-4 Phantom; he was found dead on an island; he was living in Vietnam's Central Highlands surrounded by beautiful native women. It was all too fantastic for Ray to swallow.

After bouncing and jostling for about ten minutes, and Earl scraping the bumpers against a few red pines, and each time Drift hollering, "Whoa there!" they finally came out on the blacktop, and in a short while the bridge was in sight. "Bridge to the *River Des Morts*," Earl said.

"Watch for that car, Frenchy," Ray said.

"I see it," Earl said. "Let's see if we can beat him."

"It'll be a tight squeeze," Ray said.

"I had one of those once," Earl said.

"I doubt it," said Ray.

"I'm married, remember," Earl said.

Ray flinched. "That Jeep's getting closer. Better slow down," he said, but when he looked at Earl he saw Earl had no intention of slowing down, and was swerving the pickup to scare the other driver.

"Quit screwing around," Ray said. Robby stared out the back into the darkness at Drift and red taillights. Ray remembered the sign that said *Sippery When Wet*.

Earl said, "Dumb son-of-a-bitch!" He put the truck close to the concrete railings.

"What the hell? He trying to kill us?" Ray shouted.

The Jeep came closer. Earl drove the truck up on the curb and scraped the side door and rear bed of the truck. A trail of sparks flew across the bridge. Ray felt the inward crease of metal against his thigh and smelled burning paint. Drift had hold of a bag of smelt and kept his head between his knees, as if he'd been instructed in grade school on how to survive a nuclear attack. Ray held tight to Animoosh.

The Jeep lost control on a patch of black ice, and Ray noticed the hood held down by a bungee cord. Part of the front fender dented inward and pulled out from a previous accident. The Jeep had oversized tires that stuck out beyond the wheel wells. The vehicle didn't have any doors. It hit the curb on the other side of the bridge, and went over the rail like a toy car.

"Crazy bastard!" Earl said.

ANIMOOSH

Everyone jumped out of the truck to look over the side. "Everybody okay?" Ray said. Drift waved his arms at the oncoming traffic to slow it.

Looking into the black water Robby said, "We're all right, but look…" and pointed to a young man's body pinned unnaturally against a rock, his face staring upward. Robby vomited over the bridge.

Ray went to the edge of the rail and looked below. He'd seen a young Vietnamese boy like that once when a grenade had been thrown into a NVA bunker. When two of Ray's squad members dragged the man by his legs into the blistering sun, the Vietnamese boy's arms twisted behind his neck, his legs splayed and bent at odd angles in the bloodied dirt, the eyes fixed in a head held to the boy's shoulders by a bloody thread. One of the soldiers whipped out his dick and urinated on the corpse.

There was a rushing sound in Ray's ears. It was the river. In a moment people began to move, began to take action to help the kid who was already dead. Water splashed around the Jeep that lay upside down; it swirled around the two boulders where Animoosh had almost drowned; it flowed around the young man, his limbs like weeds waving in the current.

Earl scrambled down the embankment toward the overturned Jeep, where it had come to rest against the center concrete piling. Ray followed, and they both waded into the frigid water. "Better check on the kid," Earl said. Ray pushed through the water toward the body. He was sure by this time it was a body and not a life. When he got close enough he saw there wasn't any blood, but the boy's head was twisted 180 degrees, like a doll's head. The boy's chin rested between his shoulder blades like a mask, and his eyes pulled upward, made eerie by the red flashing lights of an arriving ambulance.

"He's dead," Ray shouted.

About one hundred yards downstream, someone yelled, "They're running!" Then Ray felt a hand on his shoulder, and turned to see a Michigan State Trooper. "That's a tough one, isn't it?" Ray understood the trooper was trying to console him, but it made him nervous. "Did you find him?" the trooper asked.

"Yeah," Ray said.

"I've been a cop for a long time. Never saw anything like it."

"In Nam," Ray said. "More blood."

"It'll make it easier on his parents."

"I guess," Ray said.

"Did you know him?"

"No. . . . Didn't know him."

"I'll need a statement."

They all told the same story. They were trying to beat the Jeep across the bridge, but the kid wouldn't move. They'd tried to get out of the way, but the Jeep lost control and skidded into Earl's truck, then bounced and hit the curb on the other side of the road and flipped over the bridge. "Strangest thing," Earl said. "I don't know why he wouldn't move."

"Lots of freak things happen," the trooper said. "A Yugo with a young woman in it lost control on the Mackinaw Bridge, slid from side to side and then went over the edge. One hundred and fifty feet to the water."

"Okay," Earl said. He knew he was getting off easy. The state trooper made Earl recite the alphabet backwards and walk a straight line. Convinced he was sober enough to drive, the trooper wrote Earl a ticket for reckless driving and told him to take it easy.

Yellow wrecker lights flashed. The truck pulled onto a road next to the river. The driver got out wearing overalls. He surveyed the situation, and went to work while the crowd watched him put on his chest waders, unwind a winch cable, and pull a large hook down to the river and wrap it around the rear axle of the Jeep. A loud grinding sound came from the winch, straining against the axle and water. It was the sound of rocks and gravel being grated. Water poured from the Jeep. Down river, two EMS, a man and woman, had the boy on a stretcher inside a body bag. The ambulance turned off its lights and drove over the bridge on its way to Marquette General. Ray watched taillights disappear around a bend.

Most of the smelt fishermen had gone, the fires put out. The troopers had taken the names and addresses of witnesses. The fat man in overalls loaded the Jeep onto a trailer bed and waited for the cops to give him the go ahead.

"Harsh about the kid, eh?" Drift said. The men stood on the bridge and stared into the water.

"I thought he'd move," Earl said.

"Wasn't your fault," Ray said. "He was drunk. Had plenty of room to get out of the way. I'd like to know his blood alcohol."

"Probably read about it in the *Mining Journal*," Ray said.

"What now, boys?" Robby asked. "I'm ready to go home."

"You can take me and Robby back to the Hotel Janzen," Ray said.

"What about the smelt?" Drift asked. They looked around and for the first time noticed that the bridge was covered with dead smelt. All the bags had split open during the accident, and when the truck's tailgate popped, the smelt scattered everywhere, leaving a silver sheen on the blacktop highway.

"Don't worry, Drift," Earl said. "There's always next year."

"Won't be cleaning any fish tonight," Drift said, looking downhearted. A car passed and made a squishy sound. "When we gonna ice fish, Earl?"

Earl looked at Drift like he wanted to cuff him upside his head, but instead he said, "Not tonight, Drift. Not tonight."

In front of the Hotel Janzen a dim bulb lit the entrance of the porch where Robby, Ray, and Moosher went through the one-hundred-year-old doors; they tramped up the stairs to Jeanie's room; Ray had to see her, had to confess the night away. They heard Earl's truck roar down the street. Ray knocked on Jeanie's door. "Where's the smelt?" Jeanie said.

"Spread all over the Dead River Bridge," Ray said.

"The *River Des Morts*," Robby said, leaning with his back against the door.

"What on earth are you talking about?" Jeanie said.

"Mind if I lay down, Jeanie," Robby said. "I don't feel too good." Then he fell onto the sofa and began to snore.

Jeanie covered Robby with a blanket and said, "He don't look good, either. What'd you do to him, Ray?" She eyed the dog suspiciously.

"A little Beam," Ray said. "But there were worse things, bad things, Jeanie."

"Bad how?"

"We were trying to beat this car across the bridge. Earl thought he could make it, but this kid kept coming. His Jeep slid sideways into Earl's truck. Musta been a patch of ice. The Jeep, just like a pinball, hit the other side of the bridge and went over."

"Is he all right?"

"He got thrown from the vehicle. Ended up downstream with his neck broke. I got to him first, but I could tell he was dead. Should have seen Robby dip those smelt, though."

"Are you batty, Ray? You bring Robby to my place stone drunk, tell me a story about a dead boy, and you want to talk about stinking smelt? What is wrong with you?"

"That's not all." Ray couldn't hold back. He had to share it with Jeanie.

"What's not all?"

"The boy's head. . . ."

"Yeah?"

"It was on backwards. You know, like a doll's."

"You're not playing with a full deck, Ray."

"That's about it."

Jeanie held open the door to the hallway. "You'd better go, Ray. You look like shit."

"Feel like it."

"Don't forget your dog."

Ray left Jeanie's apartment and walked two doors down to his own room. He went straight to the cupboard and put food in Moosher's bowl. The dog sniffed at the food, and then went to a corner and curled into a ball. "Big night, eh Moosher?" Ray said. "Eat your food."

The image of the young Vietnamese soldier's face mingled with the face of the boy in the Dead River. Ray couldn't get them out of his mind. They were like rubber masks, like frowning theater masks. "Moosher," Ray called. He patted the bed, something he'd never done before. "C'mon, boy." The dog got up from his spot and climbed onto the bed. Moosher lay coiled next to Ray. He put his arms around the dog. The Dead River smell was on him, and Ray breathed it in. "Moosher," he said, and stroked the dog's head.

He worked the soft tip of the dog's ears between his fingers and wondered why Robby seemed so familiar. Then he thought about the lifeless bodies, thought about them over and over until they worried him to sleep.

TAKE ME TO THE GOLD MONKEY

All Jean had was a suitcase full of clothes and her pregnancy tucked into the back of her mind like contraband when she left Micky's Gray Street apartment and sat on the stoop to wait for Kodoski. Clouds gathered at the trees. There was a storm predicted. When her mother called, she wasn't convinced she should keep the baby and said, "Mommy I have something to tell you . . ." and before she could say anything more her mother barked like a dog into the phone. "What is it now, Mommy?" Jean said.

"I took Tiffy's blood pressure pills by mistake. I need to go to the hospital." Tiffy was a dirty brown Pug Jean's mother said drove her crazy. The dog had been an impulse buy at a pet store sandwiched between the Coney Island and Ahee's Jewelers at the Eastland Mall. Her mother bought the dog a year ago when Jean's stepfather passed, leaving her mother with a yellow brick home in Grosse Point

Park on Alter Road, a stone's throw from Detroit's city limits, where her mother could see a newly constructed Renaissance Center that reflected the sky and the Detroit River.

"I can't come now, Mommy. I'm leaving Micky. I've got to figure out where I'll live."

"Come home."

"I don't think so, Mommy."

Here she was—twenty-two years old and tired of everything: her mother's lies about her real father, living with Mickiewicz and sleeping with Randy Kodoski. Tomorrow she'd quit Polanski's Vegetable Warehouse. When she pulled her key from the lock she thought of Polanski, the owner. Always with the fruit and vegetables, holding up two ripe melons in front of his chest, stroking a cucumber. It was a distasteful ritual to everyone, and Micky was crazy jealous when she made the mistake of telling him. She'd had enough of this dream called Detroit, and wanted to wake up in a different one, where trees were pastel colors, like the bark on a sycamore, and the buildings were creamy bricks and entryways arched into portals where what you wished for came true.

Walking down three flights of stairs; the elevator didn't work, nothing worked, Jean ran her hand down the wall to keep her balance and felt the cracked plaster patching, the rise and fall of mountains and valleys. The railing wiggled like a snake. The steps squeaked under her load. The suitcase was heavy. Last week Micky caught a frenetic bat in the stairwell. They reminded her of little flying monkeys, those big ears and furry bodies. It made her dizzy, as if she'd been spun on a playground wheel, or a spell had been cast upon her.

Lucky for her Kodoski said he'd come at noon in the Checker Cab he drove, let her stay at his place until she figured things out, but when she got to the sidewalk, he was nowhere in sight. She was sure Kodoski was tired of her pissing and moaning about her real father, whom she had never known. She thought that finding her biological father might give her a sense of the real home to which she belonged and so she made phone calls to strangers with possible last names her mother gave her and had probably invented. In February, when she had eaten mushrooms, she followed a man wearing a fur hat, like a Russian might wear, and confronted him just as he stepped off a curb in front of Gabe's Bar. She touched his elbow; he jerked his arm away. "Whoa!" he said.

"Excuse me," she said. "Are you my father?" Another time she called a man and when she found out he was a Ford executive, her hopes ran high because she wanted her father to be someone interesting and important. He assured her he had never heard of her mother. Was he lying? When she told Kodoski the story, he said she needed to get a grip. At her age wondering about your real father was a waste of time—something, he said, Quixotic, a term he had learned in the only semester of college he ever attended.

"What do you mean?"

"Chasing windmills, Babe," he replied. "Look, stop romanticizing this bum. He left you and your mother, remember?"

"Maybe he didn't know I existed," Jean said.

"All the more reason to give up the quest," Kodoski said. "Besides, you're old enough to vote."

At the horizon the sky was the color of eggplant above maples and elms. Cicadas screeched in the August heat. A car crawled passed, but it wasn't Kodoski. Had he forgotten her? She'd wait.

In the stairwell to the basement apartment, someone had vomited, and the odor came up on a warm wind that shook the broad, heart-shaped Catalpa leaves. The cigar tree Micky called it because in the fall it dropped large seed pods everywhere that made Jean think of a science fiction movie, one in which her mother had been turned into something which appeared human but was not. She saw her mother burst anew from a foamy pod plant reborn. Lately, she thought, her mother's attempt to hold back time had made her look like a mannequin, a dressmaker's dummy in a flat blonde wig. Her mother's face became a lifeless moonscape of craters, and she drank too much.

Last winter she found her mother's Pinto idling behind Gabriel's bar in ten degree weather. The window was open and her mother's head lolled against the door, her hair frozen in a pointed mat. A pint bottle cradled between her legs. A thought she didn't want came to her anyway: My mother is a witch and a drunk but she is still my mother. Across Mack Avenue, a neon sign spilled emerald onto the dirty snow and pavement, and on top of the building in cursive letters: Gold Monkey. Filled with bikers, dazed hippies, and workers from the Jefferson Chrysler Plant, the Gold Monkey dancers spun on poles and put a spell on the audience. Kodoski hung out there and said the girls were not what you might assume they were, and they made good money. I could do that, Jean thought. There's still time.

That winter night her fingers found her mother's neck, the artery beat time with her own heart, and Jean felt the urge to slap her, so she did. "What?" her mother said, startled awake.

"You hate me, don't you?"

"I can't breathe," her mother said.

"You can breathe, Mommy."

"You're a pretty girl." Her mother sounded like an old lady talking to a parakeet in a pet shop: Aren't you a pretty bird? She wiped mascara from her mother's cheeks with a wetted thumb, pulled sticky puke-laced hair from the corners of her mouth.

"Move over," Jean said and slid behind the wheel.

Her mother had been this way since her step-father had been found dead and slumped over the fender of a Mustang he'd almost finished painting at the body and paint shop he owned on Gratiot Avenue. His heart, the doctor said, had exploded in his chest. Massive coronary. Jean wasn't sorry her mother sold the shop and collected the insurance. She didn't miss him or when he came into her bedroom uninvited. An odor of paint followed him. It came out of every pore in his body, as if his body were attempting to rid itself of high gloss lacquer. Though she liked to believe her bedroom was a sanctuary from her parents, it was not. The old man's money kept her mother comfortable and supplied with drink and mostly out of her life, and for that she was grateful.

After she got her mother into bed, Jean walked through the house and took whatever downers she could find. She rifled through her mother's dresser and purse and the bathroom where Tiffy had left a present on the floor she almost stepped in. She took two pills out of a prescription bottle she'd taken from the vanity and when she turned to leave, there was Tiffy. He sat on the white shag carpeting like a mud spot, and stared at her with those bulging black Pug eyes dripping mucus. He flashed his horrendous teeth. The resemblance he bore to a large bat frightened her. "What're you looking at?" she said, and dropped one of the pills in front of the dog, who immediately gobbled it up.

Two nights later she went back to the house to get the money she'd taken from her mother's purse and hid in her old bedroom inside a pillow case. The room was filled with stuffed animals on the bed, a Beatles poster on the wall, the faint odor of teenage adolescence and dog shit. Then she heard her mother's voice. She walked down the hall and into the living room. Her mother pointed at the La-Z-Boy. "Sit," she said. "Put your feet up."

"No, Mommy—"

"Yes."

Her mother pulled off her shoes and socks. Her

feet were on fire from walking one end of Polansky's to the other on the concrete floor. "These are your secondary sex organs," her mother said, referring to her breasts, and pressed at the base of her toes. Her mother had been reading books about foot reflexology, homeopathic medicine, and the New Testament. Jean figured her mother had finally gone south. It was only a matter of time. Steam from a humidifier on top of the entertainment center made curlicues around a framed print of Jesus above a TV tuned to the CBS six o'clock news. Walter Cronkite's voice filled the space and images of the Vietnam War flashed across the screen. Vicks VapoRub permeated the room. Jesus' sad eyes stared at Jean, the likeness reminding her of Kodoski, or John Lennon in bed with Yoko giving Peace a chance, the long hair, the full beard, and those captivating eyes. It felt good to have her feet massaged after standing all day waiting on customers and she was nearly asleep when her mother said, "Here are your ovaries," pressing with her thumb and forefinger on the inside of Jean's heel.

"Ouch!" said Jean.

"If you were a man this area would represent your testicles." Jean wondered how big they'd be, since it took a lot of balls to work for Polanski.

The foot massage relaxed her, and she asked her mother one more time about her father. For the first time Jean realized her mother didn't know who he was. Why hadn't this occurred to her before? "Just give me a name, Mommy," Jean pleaded. Her mother did not lack imagination, and she wasn't unintelligent. His name was Peter, she said, which seemed appropriate, given the New Testament. His friends called him Brando because he rode a motorcycle (unlikely). His name was Fernando and he was a Brazilian poet (absurd). She gave her mother credit for that last one, even though it showed she was definitely turning the bend. Jean wanted to believe her mother was nothing more than an eccentric, but in her heart of hearts, she knew eccentricity was a ruse to get others to bow before her, to do the dirty work her mother didn't want to do. Eccentrics' preferred daily tasks like cooking and cleaning be handled by someone other than themselves. Responsibility demanded a level of conscientiousness her mother did not possess.

Having a conversation with her mother was like talking to an aging movie star everyone's forgotten. "Look," her mother said, "Your real father was a decorated battle fatigued war hero who lost his first wife in an auto accident, decapitated, I think. Her last name may have been Mansfield. How could I compete with battle fatigue and decapitation? Are you satisfied now?"

When Jean looked down the block searching for Kodoski, she heard a cat's plaintive yowl or an old woman's song. The noise echoed in the alley behind the Gray Street Apartments. Shattered glass seemed to crack open the night. On the other side there was only darkness. While she waited for Kodoski, suddenly Jean saw, as if a trap door had been opened at her feet, that her mother could not tell the difference between reality and fantasy. Jane Mansfield had been killed in a car crash four years earlier, and it was falsely rumored she had been decapitated. Details printed in the Detroit Free Press would not be lost on her mother.

This is the story of my life, Jean thought—a father I'll never know, a mother in the early stages of dementia, lost inside a bottle, and a soon-to-be child. Micky was the father and when the baby was born, it would know. When the Yellow Checker Cab pulled up in front of the Gray Street Apartments, and she opened the door, a man she didn't recognize was behind the wheel. "Sorry," she said. "I thought this was my cab."

"You Jean?" the cabbie said.

"Yeah," she said.

"Kodoski's busy. Where to?"

She looked through the window at a child riding a tricycle toward her. The sun followed him. He smiled at her. She waved. "Take me to the Gold Monkey first," she said.

The cabbie looked at her in the rearview. "You got it," he said.

GONDWANA

I sit at the kitchen table with a cup of coffee, my third cigarette burning in the ashtray, and drop the clip from the Beretta 9mm onto the table and clear the chamber. The action is smooth and beautiful, well oiled, and sweet. I live in a bad neighborhood—the Cass Corridor, Midtown Detroit. I am out of the VA Hospital this time for good. Post traumatic stress disorder Dr. Morton said. You won't forget, he said. No one does. But you can forgive. Yourself. Them.

This morning I read in the *Detroit Free Press* another kid committed suicide after two tours in Iraq, another war already seven years in the making and old news. I trade coffee for a beer, Blatz because it's cheap and I've acquired a taste. I watch sunlight fade and shadows climb up the apartment next door, and see the potted geraniums Irene tends in a window box. Irene the Polish Lady from Hamtramck—the dying city. There is an odor, like cooked cabbage, rising from the alley. Irene must be eighty years old; she waves to me from her window; she waters her plants. She sings across the alley. "I'm Irene, like Goodnight Irene." I wave to her. Her son, Frank, comes once a week to check on her, but doesn't bother to hug or kiss her; he sets meager bags of groceries on her kitchen table. He is my age, middle fifties, but with a dark tan, stubble of beard and long hair over the collar of his black silk shirt, a gold cross on a chain reminiscent of Disco and cocaine. He never stays more than fifteen minutes. I've timed him, and while he's gone into another room, Irene takes soup cans and pasta, some potatoes and maybe a head of wilted lettuce or cabbage more likely from the paper bags and puts them away in her refrigerator and the lowest cupboards she can reach. The kitchen is sparse. Each time he visits, Frank takes something from a room and puts it into a paper sack Irene has emptied, but I can't make out the objects. They are too small to identify.

I have a perfect view of the alley below, of stains from who-knows-what patterned on dirty concrete like a Rorschach test. Mountains move thick with jungles, the faces of men I knew in Vietnam standing in the shadows of Motown and quad .50 caliber machine guns keeping beat with the

Jackson Five. It's today, yesterday, and thirty years ago. Their names are etched into my memory: Mr. Brown, Homeboy, Mickiewicz, and Kodoski. And yes, the dead pilot, Bobby Spendlove. Homeboy is in prison for murder, and Mickiewicz's son died in Iraq a few months back.

Before I decided not to leave my apartment, I saw Mickiewicz at the Coney Island on Lafayette Avenue two or three months ago. Half his face distorted by a stroke, a leg he dragged behind. "Fucking ambush," he said.

"Surprise attack," I said. Micky lives alone in the suburbs, and his son, Dominik, then on his second tour in Ramadi, the capital of al-Anbar Province wrote to him every day.

"I think about him all the time," Micky said. Every minute since Jean, his ex-wife, called to say Dominik wasn't his son, probably not his biological son. Micky assumed Dominik was Kodoski's child, actually knew it, and Dominik, when he became a man, suspected it too.

"Where is Jean?" I say, knowing Micky doesn't talk about her, isn't sorry she packed up a second time and moved out. That's what he says at least.

"North," Micky says. "Above the bridge."

Kodoski lives under a bridge in Biloxi, Mississippi. Homeless. Bobby Spendlove, who I only know in death, comes to me liquid and swollen. His bloated South China Sea body sits at the table across from me, his eye sockets filled with Hermit crabs I want to shoot with the Beretta. He is dressed in Navy whites. Ghosts do not forgive. Bobby says, "I died for my country."

What would I say to Micky, who lived in that old apartment on Gray Street where we cleaned Dominik's first walleye caught in Lake St. Clair at the mouth of the Clinton River. He was six years old. Kodoski was there too, and the kid's eyes went wide at the fish poured onto newsprint—slime and words smearing empty pages of war stories. It was not the protests, or Nixon's Watergate, or Huey helicopters landing on the American Embassy rooftop. It was, I remember, the Clinton River smell, the filet knife Mickiewicz used to slice under pectoral fins, the head coming away clean. Dominik's eyes full of savage wonder at the gutted fish. The copper entrails smeared across headlines: *Twelve People Die in Saigon Riots. Buddhist Monks Burn in Marketplace.*

That's some fish, boy. That was more than twenty-five years ago, the memory a bullet in my brain, the damaged synapses recalling the time it took Mickiewicz to look at his watch before he left the Coney Island and say, "One more thing," Micky says, our Chaldean waiter sweeping away ketchup and chili stained plates a few days before Micky learns of Dominik's death. "I have trouble getting my mind around these wars. Dominik sends letters, you know. He writes about pools of blood in the sand like oil, how it runs in the crevasses of broken asphalt and concrete, where Iraqi men came to buy canaries, swallows, and pigeons since time began. 'Did you know, Dad,' Dominik wrote, 'that you're looked down upon if you keep birds? A man can blow up his wife with a cell phone, but if you buy a pet, a goddamn bird, you are low class.'"

Dominik writes about howling dogs and animal carcasses, the men, women, and children bleeding in the streets. Then a woman's body explodes; she dissolves and fades to black. What can I say to Micky about this marketplace of truth? It is the only place where a dead son cannot be redeemed. There is no money back for the uneducated poor. There is no rain check for ignorance. Maybe Jean came to understand this after she learned Dominik's Humvee hit an IED, and maybe she saw that it was a never-ending cycle of men she would lose to war, even though two of them were officially alive.

Miles Davis plays the stereo and I light a pipe that glows with medical marijuana for the Hepatitis C eating my liver. "Did you use a needle in Vietnam?" my doctor asks. Of course. Transplant survival rate 93 percent.

"Gondwana" is slow and rhythmic and feels like a rain forest, like a big cat moving through bamboo shadows. Davis is a genius. Nurse's uniform is white. She gives me Charles Dickens at the Veterans Hospital, says Dickens will take me places I haven't been, introduce me to characters I may have known. You'll like Magwitch, she says. I read everything she hands me; soak it up with my eyes. These fictions are real, like the swish and swivel of her hips after she gives me the Clonazepam for anxiety. Two milligram Clonazepam makes me forget. I save them and take three or four. They are as strong as black beauties and Quaaludes.

I see the cat, or think I see her, crouched in a hunting position at the edge of a bent Ford fender half out of a garage long abandoned. Her ass twitches. She is hunting. I watch her spring from the car, a blur. White lightning. "Gondwana" thunders from the speakers. A garbage can lid clangs against a wall, a squeal the trombone sounds when Miles plays the horn, no longer concerned with technique he's long put aside in favor of intuition. I see a rat in the cat's mouth. Two kids, one black and one white come out of nowhere to chase the animal. They throw sticks and stones to break its bones. A pint bottle clips its ear and shatters. The cat crawls into a hole between two bricks. I see blood. Their laughter is elevated and wild, a shriek that bounces off brick walls. They are nine or ten, their arms linked. Urchins out of Dickens. Dirty and destitute. I'm about to shout at them, but the younger one turns and gives me the finger, like the 4-year-old boy on the side of Highway One going straight through Da Nang, taking me farther and farther north to Camp Sally and Phu Bai. I'm told we leave on patrol in forty-eight hours. I'm the new point man. Shelf life three months, but I walk for nine. My ears are born again in a rustling leaf, a sound in the otherwise still air, shadows moving through bamboo.

I stop to cut a think stem. Inside is water. I drink it. Beware of bamboo splinters. Perforated bowel. The soldiers behind me, my squad members, barely exist. I am alone and realize I will always be alone because this moment will forever define the man I cannot possibly know I will become, the man I will spend years burying with drugs and booze, waiting for the real me to emerge again from an abscess in my subconscious like a tripwired tumor. *Casualties Caused by IEDs in Afghanistan on the Rise.*

But time jumps forward, and then back. It's

then and now, the most difficult place to be, and I want to hide, to burrow through to the other side and listen to no one but me. I'm talking out loud: I'm asking Kodoski whose house we're going to for Quaaludes under the big green-leafed maples during a Detroit summer. At someone's home near Alter Road we're walking in the glow of yard lights shiny on the waxed underside of Grosse Point plants. They don't have names. I am already in an upside down world of weed and beer, anticipating the ludes I'll feel in my esophagus when I dry swallow. My eyes feel red-rimmed. In six months I lose thirty pounds. I weigh one hundred and twenty-three. Man, I'm hot as Willy Peter skyrocketing through a too dark sky for stars when we score and drive to Gabe's Bar. I lose Kodoski. The ludes numb me in white phosphorescence. They make me jabber. Words tumble from my mouth. Jibber–jabber. Even I would prefer not to hear them. I tell the girl checking IDs she's a bitch. She says we're all losers. You Vietnam vets are losers. The only feature she has in her face is a mouth. When she opens it, I think of my cock there, but all is black space, a snaked tongue between ruby lips and long white teeth. Bad omen. "Fuck you, girl," I say, stepping outside to look for Kodoski. I'm angry but I'm not sure why, so

I kick a brick wall. "Fuck it, fuck you," I say to the bouncer who says I have to leave. I'm already gone and take a swing. He's much taller, a former Golden Gloves. He grabs my wrist and spins me around. I hit the building. He hits me twice in the gut. I'm out of my body now, watching my knees buckle to the greasy sidewalk. Look at that idiot, I think, he doesn't know the destiny of his own ass-kicking. Kodoski brakes his battered truck in front of Gabe's. "Get in," he says, sees I'm badly beaten. "I'll kill him," he says.

"Forget it," I say. We roar in Kodoski's pick up east to Jefferson Avenue. I'm barely conscious.

What would I do without Nurse? She wipes drool from the corner of my mouth, tells me it's time for my appointment with Dr. Morton. This is last year or the year before, or the year before that? I don't cry anymore. I tell Morton instead about my grandfather and his big metal fishing box. Trays fold out three to a side. Plastic leeches are soaked in Oil of Anise, the faint smell of liquorice and fennel rising out of the box. Good memories of bobbers and sinking lures, floaters, night crawler harnesses, monofilament, a knife my grandfather made at the River Rouge Ford Plant. *The hardest steel comes from the hottest fire*. Grandfather says he doesn't feel well. "It's very hot," he says. "Too hot."

I telephone a doctor in a small town called Caseville ten miles north.

"What's he doing?" the doctor says. Why I didn't take him to the emergency room escapes me. Was there a reason? Was there an emergency room? Was this a crisis? "Just watch him," is the doctor's best medical advice. I tell Morton about my grandfather because grandfather is naked and dead in a red plush chair on a day in early August when I'm seventeen and it feels like my fault. The humidity chokes me. Grandfather is eighty-four. It is my first encounter with the dead. An ambulance arrives and three of us lift him onto the gurney. He's heavier than stone.

"What would happen if you didn't think it was your fault?" Morton says.

I want to answer with a story about walking behind grandfather at the mouth of a river, following him onto Lake Huron. Therapy reveals my life to me in one hour increments, and there isn't much time if you believe Time to be a reality. The hours pass quickly. Eventually I will tell Morton I'm falling faster than my arms can catch me. My chin hits first, blood splatters on black ice. I'm running behind grandfather, trying to catch him, leaving drops of blood patterned like a wounded animal loping across a frozen desert of ice, a coyote maybe or wolf, a bear from a book of poems by Galway Kennel that nurse leaves near my bed. Grandfather enters the fishing shanty growing farther from me, a small lantern light on a prairie of snow.

"Is this a dream?" Morton says.

"Of course," I say. It's the correct answer. When I think about grandfather everything is frozen, the swamp at the mouth the river, the cattails that poke out of the snow like cornstalks, the lake I tell Morton I sometimes wish I'd fall into and drown. "It's a sweet death," I tell him.

"What do you mean?" Morton says.

Irene is at the window, waving at me, her palms smooth like wax, parchment skin paper thin. "I'm going to see my sister today in Mt. Clemens," she shouts, "Frank is taking me," as if Mt. Clemens were a faraway place fifteen miles north, a city of one-hundred-year-old sulfur baths, and air breathed deeply by the prosperous and those made affluent by selling simple pleasures: inhaling brine and steam. I wave to Irene.

Morton doesn't raise his eyebrows or shift in his chair when I tell him mother was institutionalized at the Pontiac State Hospital. She's catatonic and sits on the edge of her bed three years after my sister's death at seven weeks. Morton never reacts. "You're not crazy," he says.

GONDWANA

At the Pontiac State Hospital steel bars drip from windows where my mother is kept, and I ask father why my mother is there. He tells me those floors are for sick people who commit crimes. My father's mouth is a line drawn tight across his face. Mother stands on a step leading to the building, raises a limp hand in a gesture that is either hello or goodbye, brushes away a fly much in the same manner she'll cover her vagina on her death bed twenty years later when I visit her at Detroit General Hospital, and sit near her side, wishing she would die and end our suffering. The doctors say she doesn't know me; she's brain dead, organs failing, but not her dignity. On the long drive home, grandfather isn't even there. He's gone to Van Nuys, California, to see his sister, to fish the ocean from a long pier he later tells me juts far into the sea, far enough to catch sharks, he says.

At the mention of sharks, Bobby Spendlove floats up on the light blue kitchen linoleum patterned with grimy sea shells and coral when I least expect him. What have I done with my life? What would Bobby Spendlove do with his had he been the one to find me floating in the South China Sea, forever alive in his thoughts instead of mine?

Guilt manifests itself in the combat soldier as it

does for the worker who keeps his job while others are laid off, Morton tells me. The information isn't useful, and sometimes I believe Morton gives me theories he's only read in a book rather than experienced. I try to explain to him that I didn't know this pilot, Bobby Spendlove, anymore than I know Irene, an old lady across the alley who sips tea, and whose son, I suspect, is stealing her memories. I can only watch from a window of an apartment paid for with government money. Blood money. I cannot leave or walk through that door no more than Spendlove can rise from sand and water where Mr. Brown and Homeboy find him in his algae-caked helmet, his casket closed when he arrives home on a C-130 filled with dead men and women, flags draped the length of aluminum coffins lighter than a case of beer if not for the lifelessness of the marbled dead.

Spendlove—his mother's only consolation the image of her once alive son. The time he came home and told her he'd enlisted in the Navy. The moment he threw his cap in the air when he'd graduated from the Naval Academy, and when he stood in his high chair and fell forward, and she caught him midair before he hit the floor. She'll hear his voice tonight, and thirty years later will remember how she checked to see if he was breathing when they brought his infant body home from the hospital. After several years pass, his father, a World War II veteran, will realize his son died for a notion in which he, himself, once believed. Morton is sympathetic, admits he understands these ideas no better than I do when I ask: For what?

The shadows grow like broad-leafed vines up brick walls across the alley. It's getting dark, the night punctuated by flickering streetlamps, the drunken lamps of memories I want to extinguish, but I believe something, a revelation that might set ablaze gas lanterns of my imagination disappearing down a ninetieth-century London street, one by one lighting the way, and then tell me what's hidden in the shadows. Charles Dickens is too much on my mind. It will be a relentless night. The open refrigerator lights the room. I rub a can of Blatz across my forehead; I hold the beer can against my throbbing temple, against the fire burning like napalm on a ridge just two hundred yards distant and down my throat. The sticky tear-shaped gel freezing on tree limbs, on the charred body of an NVA soldier caught in mid-scream his beloved will never hear.

Irene passes a window. Her movements are hesitant in the conscious effort the elderly make not to fall. She shuffles across the floor as if hovering above it. I see her sit in a ladder-backed chair, cards spread before her on a wooden table in solitaire. Today, like each day, she is there, the old Polish lady who sings to me across the alley. Her cellophane hand flips each card. She is opaque in the light, an apparition.

Her son, Frank, is there too. He moves about the room solid and purposeful opening drawers and removing tableware. He drapes clothes from closets over his arm, fills boxes with dishes. He's wearing sunglasses in the darkened room. Is Irene moving, leaving me? How come Irene ignores him? He wraps plates and bowls in newspaper. Irene's garments are dumped into a plastic tub on the kitchen table. She doesn't let Frank disrupt her game; she doesn't seem to notice him. Frank winds tape around cartons stacked against the kitchen wall. He pours water from a heated pan into a cup and drinks from it; he doesn't make tea for his mother. The cupboards are open and bare. The drawers stick out like tongues. Then Frank reaches over his mother's head and turns out the lamp hanging over the table. A crack of light fills the room when he leaves the apartment. Then he shuts the door. He leaves her in the dark. There's something wrong. I can't see Irene in the blackened room. Maybe she needs help. I slide the magazine back into the Beretta and chamber a round; I wait in the dark. Goodnight Irene.

THE AUTHOR

 A high school graduate from a suburb on Detroit's Eastside, Allen Learst grew up believing he was destined to work for the auto industry. At 18, he took a job at the Chrysler Tank Plant; later, after Vietnam, where he served as a combat infantryman in the 101st Airborne Division, he worked for the Ford Motor Company Interior Plant. Factory life, however, didn't agree with him, so he took advantage of his G.I. Bill and began his education at Macomb Community College. He earned a BS and MA from Northern Michigan University in Marquette, Michigan, and a PhD in Creative Writing from Oklahoma State University in Stillwater, Oklahoma. Before and during his college years he had more than twenty blue collar jobs. Before returning to school to complete his doctorate, he also worked at the U.S. Fish and Wildlife Service. He is now a Senior Lecturer at the University of Wisconsin in Marinette, Wisconsin.

LINKS

Visit Leapfrog Press on Facebook
Google: Facebook Leapfrog Press

Leapfrog Press Website
www.leapfrogpress.com

Author Website
www.allearst.com

About the Type

This book was set in Bembo, a typeface modeled on those cut
by Francesco Griffo for Aldus Manutius in 1495 in Venice, Ita-
ly. Griffo's design is considered one of the first of the old style
typefaces, which include Garamond, that were used as staple
text types in Europe for 200 years. Stanley Morison supervised
the design of Bembo for the Monotype Corporation in 1929.

Designed by John Taylor-Convery
Composed at JTC Imagineering, Santa Maria, CA